Through the Curtain

THRILLER ROMANCE

Patrick Connelly

Book and Cover design by Astounding Stories
ISBN: 978-1-68204-320-2

First Edition: September 2016

10 9 8 7 6 5 4 3 2 1

Introduction

Thank you so much for purchasing this book.

Sign up and Join our Review Team – every time we publish new book we will send you ARC (Advance Reader Copy) so you can read and post honest review for that book!

(Click the link or enter http://astounding-stories.com/romancereviewteam into your browser.)

Through the Curtain
MYSTERY THRILLER ROMANCE

by Patrick Connelly

Chapter 1

Inayah whimpered softly, hidden behind the veil of her niqab. Her eyes glistened with her tears, so anyone who sincerely was interested would know that she was crying. She hated tears. They were a sign of weakness, but still, the tears filled her eyes. A bomb had come too close this time. The blast took the face off the building across the street from her house. Her father had demanded that she and her mother hide immediately in the closet. No one could see her tears there in the dark. Her father left them and went to the headquarters of the Special Forces of the Iraqi army. He was a major and as such, he was expected to appear ready for service whenever needed, but especially when a bomb exploded so close to headquarters. His new recruits would be there waiting for him, though none of them would be known by their real name of ISIS, at least, not up front.

The Major bounded in through the door of the bustling headquarters and was immediately bombarded by information and questions. He was a squat middle-aged man with a very black moustache and an equally jet-black beard and extreme intense black eyes that peered over a very long sharp pointed nose. His mouth was set in a permanent grimace. His Arabic tongue, flawless. He barked out orders and pointed on a map, sending his men out across the city with orders to bring back the culprits who set that bomb: dead or alive. He was approached by one of his three secretaries.

"The American Ambassador has asked for a meeting, Mohammed." His subordinate handed him a stack of papers. "Shall I set the meeting?"

His answer was quick and deliberate, "Meeting denied."

In his home his wife and daughter were huddled together in the closet, waiting for him to return and tell them that 'all was clear' and that they could come out of the dark cold closet. Inayah prayed silently. She didn't want to upset her mother, but without warning her tears formed in her eyes and she cried softly. This had been her life for so long, she knew she should be used to the disruption, but every time her father sent them to the closet, she felt death coming closer. Her panic made her heart beat against her chest and she felt a chill run rampant through her body. Her knees were folded up under her chin and she could hear her mother's frightened breath coming out in spurts of puffs of anguish. Neither woman spoke.

Hours passed and the two women, the mother and her twenty-year old daughter, stayed hidden in the closet, not knowing if the enemy would come bounding into their home at any second; not knowing who that enemy might be. As the hours went by, Inayah began to feel a powerful deep energy within herself. Her thoughts became bolder than they had ever been. She no longer wanted to be a sheep. She put her arm around her mother and pulled her close. She vowed she would no longer be the victim.

They heard the front door open. They heard boots on the wooden floor. Inayah held her breath.

The door was pulled abruptly open. The light flooded the small enclosure and made her eyes blink. A man in full military uniform with his gun clutched in his hand stood outlined in the bright light. "Come with me," he ordered. His accent was slightly different and Inayah sensed evil in his words.

Inayah helped her mother to her feet and kept her hand under her mother's elbow to steady her. Then, when she saw the insignia on the young man's uniform confirming her fears, she slipped the knife from under her skirt quickly, like a farmer with a scythe cutting wheat, she brought it up and slit the man's throat from right to left. Her mother gasped. The man fell to the floor. A hot rush consumed Inayah's body. She thought she would feel a sense of regret or remorse, but all she felt was satisfaction. She glanced at the man's open eyes as he faced his mortality.

She glanced around the room. The man was alone.

"Grab his legs." She instructed her mother as she also grabbed one leg and began to drag the man into the closet. She closed the door quickly. Her eyes saw the bright red streak of blood leading up to the closet door. She ran into the kitchen to get a towel and a bowl of water. She mopped up the blood and then went back into the kitchen and hurriedly washed out the cloth and the bowl. Her mother was frozen as she watched her daughter's movements. "Now come," Inayah took her mother's hand. They went out the back door and scurried like two crabs down the narrow alley. Her father had told her where she should go if their hiding place was ever breached. She led her mother through the streets. There were very few people venturing out of their homes after the bomb scare, so she knew if she did see someone she should be aware. Finally, they reached the destination. She slid open the heavy steel cover of the street drain. She helped her mother onto the ladder and watched as she climbed safely down into the dark hole. Inayah's eyes scanned the street for anyone who might be watching, but there was no one in the street. She slid the heavy cover over her head as she descended the ladder into the dark hole below her. She almost cursed when her foot caught in her niqab. She kept her grip tightly on the rails of the ladder. Her foot sought the solid ground. She whispered, "Mother are you near?" Her mother's hands reached out in the blanket of black and touched her daughter.

"I am here, Inayah."

Inayah grabbed onto her mother's hand and turned left in the tunnel. She walked carefully, feeling the slime of the water under her shoes. She kept a tight grip on her mother as they wound into the tunnel, turning exactly as her father had told her to do. Right, right, left, right. Her hands often sought the dank slime-covered walls to guide her. She kept the format clear in her mind. Left, left, left, right, left, right. She had memorized the exit formula for years. Even as a little child her father had sat her on his knee making a song of the formula of escape. Finally, she felt a solid wall on all sides. "This is it," she told her mother. She reached out in front of her until her hands hit the solid wall with the railings of a ladder. "I will go up first, to be sure it is safe to exit." She slowly climbed up the ladder. She hit her head on the metal plate at the top. She pushed the steel plate, but it did not move. She banged with the heel of her hand, but still the plate held firmly, from years of sealing the tunnel. She took her knife from under her skirt and pried along the edge of the covering, feeling first with her fingers, and then sliding the knife. She pushed again and felt the lid give way. She slid it slowly to the left. A small ray of light hit her eyes. "Come mother." She called down. Her mother began her ascent towards the small sliver of light. The room was tiny with benches for sitting, but no more than that. The daughter and her mother sat down on a bench to wait.

Hours passed. Inayah heard the growl of her stomach. She had committed an oversight. She brought no food or water. She and her mother could be in this room for days. She cursed herself for not thinking about the human needs. Her mother slept and leaned on her daughter's shoulder. Inayah did not sleep. Her eyes were wide and her ears perked at any sound. She must be vigilant. Her mother stirred. "Inayah, how much longer?" she asked.

"Soon mother. Soon." But in truth, Inayah had no idea when her father would come. She only knew that they must not leave this room. She had no idea where they were or what laid beyond this room. Her eyes, now accustomed to the dim light looked around the room. There was nothing, except for four walls and the twelve benches. She wondered if the benches were ever filled with people. She wondered how long they could stay alive without water or food. She wondered if she could reverse the formula and go back to their kitchen to retrieve food and water if she needed to do so. Her mother squeezed her arm, "We should not have come." She said in a shaking voice.

"It will be fine, mother. Father will come soon, Inshallah. Pray." Yet as the hours passed slowly by, she began to wonder if, indeed, God was willing that her father would come. Twenty-four hours passed. Her mother was now laying on the floor, her head on her arm, her legs curled up under her niqab, sleeping. Still, her daughter did not sleep. Her eyes were wide and her mind continued to race. She second guessed her decision to come to the hiding place. Maybe she should have taken her mother to their Uncle's house instead. Thoughts of doubt raked at her mind. The crack of light from the window faded into dark again. Inayah thought about going back to their house more and more. She began to try to retrace the formula.

When the sun came peeking through the cracks of the boarded up window for the second time, Inayah began to worry. Not for herself, but for her mother. She hadn't been well lately and two days without food and water certainly were not a good thing for her. "Mother, I'm going to try to go back to our house to get some food and water."

Her mother clung to her and began to cry. "No, don't leave me. Your father will be here soon. We can wait." Her tears began to soak through her niqab. "Inayah, please." She begged.

Inayah touched her mother's hand, "Don't be afraid, mother. You must be brave. We don't know how long we must wait here. We cannot go outside of this room and I was thoughtless in not bringing water and food." She shook her head, "How could I be so stupid?"

No sooner had the words left her mouth then a door opened and her father was standing before her. At first she was frightened and reached for her knife, but then she saw his smile. "Father! It's you."

"Who else would it be? Come, we must hurry." He turned and led them into a courtyard. They began to follow a guide until they came upon a car. The guide handed the keys to her father. He also handed him a map and three canteens of water.

The guide whispered, but Inayah could hear his words. "The American will meet you at the spot on the map marked by an x."

She helped her mother into the backseat. She took one of the canteens and gave it to her mother. The older woman began to drink quickly, gulping the water, then when she had her fill, she lay across the seat and closed her eyes. Inayah went around the car and got into the passenger seat in front. She kept her eyes straight ahead as she waited for her father to get in the car. Out of the corner of her eye she saw the quick movement of her father's arm, a jerk of his arm, a flash of steel, then the guide fell to the ground. She continued to watch straight ahead, but saw her father carry the body to the bushes. He bent over the body and dug in the pockets of the shirt and pants, procuring all the contents. He then shoved the papers, wallet, and miscellaneous things into his own pockets. Her father got into the driver's seat and started the engine. He glanced at the gauges to make sure that there was enough gas and that all systems were working properly. Then, he turned the wheel sharply and left the courtyard via an open gate. She did not speak to her father. His eyes were sharply tuned to the road ahead of them. When dusk fell, he turned on the headlights and kept driving. He stopped only once at a crossroads and opened the map. He put it on the seat beside him and then turned right. The shadows of the night seemed to haunt their passage. Inayah glanced into the backseat and saw that her mother was sleeping, but she did not close her eyes. She watched the road ahead of them as if she herself was driving. Her father never spoke.

Hours passed before her father stopped the car and turned to her and said, "No more gas. We walk from here. Get your mother."

She nodded and got out of the car and opened the back door. She gently shook her mother's shoulder. "Mother, come we must walk from here." Her mother did not move. She shook her shoulder with more determination. "Mother, come!" Fear began to creep into her thoughts. "Mother? Mother!" Her mother did not move.

"Father! Father! Something is wrong with mother." She screamed for her father, forgetting that they had a dire need to be silent.

He came around to her side of the car and leaned into the car. He shook his wife's shoulder. He put his face close to his wife's face. "She's dead." He said bluntly. "We have to go Inayah. We have to leave her."

"What? She can't be dead." Inayah pushed past her father and lifted her mother's torso up off the seat and cradled her in her arms. "Mother! No!" She began to rock her mother in her arms, "No, no, no," she repeated. She felt her father's fingers close on her shoulder.

"Inayah, we have to go now. There is no time. They will take your mother to her brother. We cannot wait any longer. Come." He yanked on her shoulder and pulled her from the car, letting her mother's body fall back onto the seat. "Inayah, you know we have to leave or we will be killed. Do you want to die?"

She looked into her father's black eyes. She turned her head to look at her mother, wondering briefly why no tears were falling from her eyes. She followed her father into the woods. His pace was grueling and she found herself puffing as she tried to keep up with him. She watched him adjust the straps of the two guns over his shoulder. She thought, *Where had he found the guns?* Then she remembered that he had opened the trunk. Of course, that is where the guns were stored. When he stopped to rest she was grateful as she caught her breath.

She whispered, "Father, may I carry one of the guns?"

He turned and looked at her, his eyes taking in her niqab and then staring into her eyes. He paused, as if he was thinking of all the possibilities, good and bad. He handed her one of the guns. "Do you know how to use it?" He asked.

She nodded as she put the strap over her shoulder. They continued to trudge through the woods, climbing over fallen logs and piles of dried leaves. "Father where are we going?" She finally managed to ask.

He stopped walking and turned towards her. "The Zagros Mountains. Then from there to the Persian Gulf." He sat down on a log. "We will rest now. There is time. I don't believe we are followed."

"Followed? Where are we going?" She rarely spoke to her father, let alone ask him questions, but here in the middle of the forest she felt less his daughter, or a mere woman, she felt she had earned her passage. She killed a man; he killed a man and they had left her mother dead in a car— and a gun was slung over her shoulder.

His eyes once again stared at her. It was as if he was trying to figure out by looking into her eyes if he could trust her. She thought, *I am his daughter and he doesn't trust me? What kind of father is this? Who is this man?*

He sat down on a log. She joined him at the other end of the log. .He finally answered, "We are meeting an American."

Her eyes widened.

He nodded, "Yes, we meet him tomorrow and he will take us out of Iraq."

She tried to digest what he was saying. They were leaving the country of her birth? Where were they going? Why were they going? She didn't ask him any of her questions. She watched him stand again.

"We must go." He began to walk away. She continued to sit on the log. Was her father a traitor? She didn't move.

"Inayah!" His voice raised.

She stood up slowly. He motioned with his hand for her to follow as he began to walk again. She willed her feet to move, but they felt as if they were glued to the ground. Her thoughts raced through her mind. *I don't know this man. Who is this man? Should I trust him?* Fear rose up like bile in her throat. She dare not cross him now. She saw how ruthlessly he killed their guide, but then she thought of how her knife had so easily slit the neck of the man who opened the closet door; it had been so easy, like a knife sliding through butter. Her foot lifted and she followed him.

They came to a dirt road. There parked with its front bumper pointing west was an old blue pick-up truck. Her father slowed his steps and put his finger to his lips as a signal for her to be quiet. He circled to the right and motioned for her to move to the left. She took the strap off her shoulder and held the gun out in front of her as she followed his lead. He pointed to the truck and then he made a motion that told her to keep her eyes opened. Then, they heard a voice call out. "Mohammed, I'm your point. Who's that you have with you? No one said there would be more than one."

Mohammed called out, "This is my daughter, Inayah. She will travel with me."

"I was told there would be only one." The voice called out from somewhere in the woods.

"It is my daughter and I or nothing." Her father answered.

She let out a sigh. Her thoughts tumbled together, *This man IS my father!* She felt a leap of her heart. *He will not turn on me.* She pointed her gun toward the voice.

"Alright then, get in the truck and I will join you." The voice called out again.

Her father shook his head, "No, you get into the truck first," he ordered.

"Listen Mohammed there is protocol and protocol says you have to get into the truck before I do."

Mohammed did not move. He waited. "I won't get in before you." He called out.

They both waited. A man came out of the woods and headed towards the truck. He opened the driver's door and got in. He put both his hands on the wheel as a sign of safety. Mohammed and Inayah approached from two different sides. When they got to the truck, Mohammed yanked the door open with his gun pointed at the man behind the wheel.

"Listen, Mohammed, this is legit. You have no worries. I'm here to take you to the boat and from there a helicopter will take you to Germany and from there to the United States. It's as simple as that. No big double cross." Mohammed stared at the man's face. He was obviously special ops.

"Are you alone out here?" Mohammed glanced into the woods.

"Yep." The man smiled. He was wearing a green baseball cap and a blue sweatshirt. "I've been waiting for you for three days."

"There were problems." Mohammed motioned for Inayah to come to the truck. She had been waiting for his signal. He pointed to the back of the truck. She struggled to get into the bed, but managed to pull herself up and get in. Mohammed slid into the seat on the passenger side. "Okay, we're ready."

The man in the baseball cap grinned, "Well, okay then. It's off to America." He started the engine and drove speedily down the dirt road leaving a trail of dust behind them. Every now again he skid into a curve, but he never let up on the gas. Finally, they saw a blue expanse of water before them. "Your boat will be waiting to take you to the helicopter pad. You will travel by helo to Germany."

Mohammed nodded.

When the truck finally stopped, he got out of the truck. For a moment he thought of killing the driver, but then thought better of it. No use making the Americans angry. Inayah got out of the truck bed. She slid down the fender. She caught her niqab on the bumper and they all heard the loud ripping sound. She looked down and saw that there was a jagged rip exposing her leg. She looked from her father's eyes to the torn dress.

"Come on," he said gruffly. She followed him with her head down, clutching the gun close to her body.

Everything was a blur, from the ride on the boat to the helicopter pad, to the American Army base in Germany and then onto the airplane with their tickets in hand. She sat next to her father and did not speak. A man in a black suit sat next to her at the end of their three-seat row. She saw his eyes briefly look at her father. Her father nodded.

The flight was long. Passengers behind them coughed, sneezed, got up and went to the bathroom, but she did not move. She didn't close her eyes. She looked straight ahead. She could feel her knife pushing into the side of her leg. No one had made them go through a check point machine. *So much for American security*, she thought. She saw her father's hands interlocked on his lap. She knew he would also have a knife on him. Their guns had been taken from them when they got on the helicopter. Her father had protested, but eventually the Americans won. They had refused to let them board if they didn't give up the guns.

When the plane flew over Washington, DC, she saw the monuments lit up below them. She had read about Abraham Lincoln in a book. There he was, larger than life, all lit up in a domed room. The city looked beautiful with all the lights and even though it was late at night people were in the park. Kids were even roller skating. She saw the runway and wondered how such a huge plane could land on such a short runway! She gasped when they began the plane's descent. She saw the water coming closer and closer. Her father did not seem moved by any of it. He kept looking straight ahead. The man next to her checked his seatbelt, so she did the same. The plane landed smoothly and all the passengers clapped their hands.

They waited until everyone was off the plane and then the man on the end of their row stood. He nodded towards her father. Her father stood, so she stood. They followed the man out of the plane. When they got to the tunnel into the airport, her father walked behind the man and she followed closely behind.

They were taken to a small room in the airport marked "Security" on the door. Her father had sat in silence as the man behind a desk spoke. "There is no love here for you, Mohammed. It is a matter that you are an excellent soldier for your country and we saw that you were beginning to train young recruits. That's why we approached you. I'll be honest with you, Mohammed, we would rather you worked for us than train young boys to become monsters within ISIS."

Her father didn't comment. She wondered what ISIS was. She wondered why the man behind the desk had a stack of papers at least four inches thick in front of him. "This is your file, Mohammed. We will close it and mark it 'secret'. All you have to do is blend into life in America. Are you prepared to do that?"

The stuffy air seemed to become even heavier as they waited for her father to answer. He looked down at his hands. Inayah knew he still had his knife under his clothes, just as she had hers. If he gave her the sign they would jump on this man together and stab him before he could make a sound. But her father gave no such sign. He was very quiet. In the quiet she could feel his agitation.

"My wife," he said slowly.

"I'm so sorry, sir. We found her body and we will make sure she gets a proper burial. Her brother has been notified." The man continued to stare at her father. "Can you blend into life in America, Mohammed?"

Her father did not blink. He nodded.

"Good. And what about your daughter?" The man smiled and looked at Inayah.

"She will learn to speak better English."

The man laughed, "Like you? You don't even have an accent."

It was true. Her father spoke clear, perfect English, without a hint of an accent. He had spent years in American colleges, but Inayah didn't know this at the time. She had studied English, but she found it a waste of time, until now.

"We have found your sister, Mahibah." The man reached into a drawer and took out a set of keys. He threw them across the desk and they landed in front of her father. "Your new apartment is in Alexandria next door to your sister. I trust you will be comfortable. It isn't fancy, but it is a roof.

We will expect you to report to Langley as soon as possible once you are settled in. We have provided you with basic needs in your apartment." The man closed the file in front of him and slapped his hand on the folder's cover. "So, that's that, then."

Her father stood, so she stood. He still didn't speak, but turned to leave the room. The man behind the desk spoke once more, "Just remember, Mohammed, we'll be watching you."

They were driven to their new apartment. The apartment was in a run-down tenement building near old Alexandria. The driver opened their doors so they could get out and then he quickly drove off leaving them on the curb. Her father walked slowly up to the purple door. He used the key the man had given him to open it.

The small room had a chair, a couch, and a television. They walked down a short hallway. They looked to the right and saw a room with a double bed, a side table with a lamp. They walked a few steps further and looked to the left and saw the small kitchen with a four-burner gas stove, a small table with two chairs, and one set of low hanging cupboards. They walked down the hallway a few steps more and found another bedroom on the right with a twin bed, a nightstand, and a small dresser. At the end of the hall was a bathroom. The shower was stained with brown water stains, as well as the sink and toilet.

Her father pointed to the room with the twin bed. "Yours." He said.

She went into the tiny bedroom and slowly closed the door. She went to the window and opened it an inch for some fresh air. The window panes were crusted with dirt, but she could still see outside into the street. She debated if she should close the window and lock it to be safe, but then decided that she didn't care if anyone tried to come in. She would kill them...

The whole scene seemed so long ago now. Iraq was a million miles away. The small closet now had three clean niqab hung on hangers. The small dresser contained her underwear and socks. The room was now familiar and comfortable. When she came into it she felt safe and at peace. She glanced at the small pink heart pillow on the white bedspread on her bed. *This is home,* she thought. She reached down and lifted the pillow to her chest. She often marveled that she felt this way, but not only did she have everything she needed, she had her Aunt Mahibah right next door. She missed her mother terribly and somehow, Mahibah filled the void in her heart. Her father was gone more than he was home, so in many ways she enjoyed her new found freedom, even though that freedom was within the confines of the small shabby apartment.

It was idyllic. She read books that her aunt brought to her and listened to her aunt's stories. But then, one night her father came home drunk.

He began to holler at her, "You are nothing but a whore!" He screamed and slapped her face. Then he reached into a drawer in the kitchen and took out a wooden spoon. He began to beat on her back and her legs. "Your mother is dead and you are nothing to me! Nothing! I waste my money feeding your face!" He roared. Inayah did not cry. The blows stung and cut into her skin, but she would not give him the pleasure of her screams, so he beat her harder. "Why were you even born? Your mother is dead and you live because you didn't take care of her. You let her die." He beat on her back with the wooden spoon harder. She thought of the knife hidden under her clothes, but she didn't take it out. After some minutes he stopped when his arm grew tired. She had fallen to her knees in front of him as he continued to beat upon her back, but now the blows stopped. He collapsed on the couch. "Get out of my sight!" he screamed at her. She backed away on all fours until she had made it to the door of her room. She backed into the room and pulled herself up with the assistance of the door knob. She fell onto the bed, blood soaking through her niqab onto the white bedspread.

He was right, she thought, I let my mother die because I wasn't prepared. I didn't think it through. It should have been me dead on the backseat of that car. I deserve every blow of that wooden spoon. But she didn't cry. She lay very still and felt the pain waves roll through her body. When he left for work in the morning she would shower and attend her wounds. For now, she lay there looking at the peeling ceiling. She forced her mind to lock out any more thoughts, other than, I deserve those blows. I deserve to be beaten.

In the shower the next morning she saw the cuts all over her body and the huge welts and bruises. She let the hot water run over her for some time. She let her long hair become drenched with the water and shampooed it with the last of the hair shampoo. When she got out she stared at herself in the long cracked mirror behind the door. Her body was an ugly mass of purple and black. She whispered, "Thank God he didn't beat my face."

Aunt Mahibah was horrified when she saw the marks on her niece's body. "I will speak with him," she announced boldly.

"No Aunt Mahibah, I deserved it. I let my mother die due to my negligence. Father is right to beat me."

"He was drunk, Inayah. This is not justice. It is not allowed in America. Men cannot beat their wives or their children. It is against the law." Her Aunt reached out and touched her niece's face which was hidden under her niqab. "Just like this niqab. You are young, you should not have to wear this in America."

"But Aunt, you wear your niqab."

"Ach! I am old. My husband is old. He doesn't care what I do, but I wear it out of respect for him." She smiled and Inayah saw that some of her aunt's teeth were missing.

"Did your husband beat you?" Inayah asked.

Her aunt was silent. Then she said, "My husband and my father. It is the Arabic women's lot in life. We were born to men who punish us for the least of any infraction." She raised her bent finger in the air, "But not here in America. If my husband beat me here, I would report him to the authorities and he knows it." Her voice was firm. "I will speak to your father."

"But won't it make him even angrier?"

Her aunt shook her head, "It will make him wiser. First of all, he should not drink. This is against Islam. Second of all, this is America. He lives here now. I am sure the authorities would not like to have him beating his daughter."

Inayah turned away from her aunt. She inhaled deeply, "It won't happen again." She felt her knife pushing into her thigh. Her aunt had opened her eyes. Yet, deep in her heart she felt the pangs of sadness. She truly believed that she had failed her mother. "I did fail my mother."

"Your mother was ill for a very long time, Inayah. She wrote me a letter, here let me find it." The older woman began to dig in a drawer in the kitchen. She lifted a thin piece of paper in the air. "Here." She unfolded it and began to read, "I have not told my husband or Inayah, but I am very ill. I feel that I will not make it through the year. I have such pains that capture my body and make me cry out." She paused to look into Inayah's eyes. "So you see, dear niece, your mother knew she was dying. You did not kill her."

Inayah thought, *It was a night of killing,* but she said nothing more to her aunt.

"You need to take that niqab off your head, at least in my presence." Her aunt instructed her. "Pull it down. Let me see your hair."

Inayah obeyed and pulled it off her head. Her aunt smiled, "Oh, such beautiful honey colored hair! Oh and see how the lights reflect from it and the lights in your eyes are made even brighter." She reached out her hand and ran it down the smooth slick long hair. She curled it around her fingers, "You are beautiful, Inayah."

Inayah blushed a bright pink. "You are too kind, aunt." She glanced at the clock on the wall, "Oh I need to get home before my father. I should have his dinner ready for him."

"But Inayah, most times he doesn't even come home for dinner. Why do you bother to prepare until he arrives?"

Inayah covered her head once again. "He's my father, Aunt Mahibah. I do it out of respect." She opened the door and slipped out into the street and then turned right to go to the apartment next door. She stared at the purple door. No one else had such a hideous purple door. Most of the doors were black or white, but there it was, the bright purple door. She unlocked it and went in. Her father was sitting on the couch. He looked at her with his dark eyes.

"Are you alright?" He asked.

She nodded and hurried into the kitchen to prepare his dinner.

The days passed slowly as Inayah read book after book that her aunt gave her. Some were books she purchased at the used book store and some were books from the library. Sometimes Inayah read them aloud to practice her English, but most of the time she would curl up on her bed and read for hours and hours. But then, she heard a deep voice right outside her window. She went to the window sill and sat down on the floor; She pulled aside the curtain, keeping her fingers tightly closed around it. She put her ear close to the one-inch gap that she always left for fresh air to come in. She could hear the male voice on his cell phone. He was walking back and forth in the little alley in front of the apartments across from hers. If she opened her window wide, she could reach out and touch him.

He walked back and forth as he spoke, at times almost touching her window. "Yes, I know. Well, I am going to try to get the weekend off so we can go to Atlantic City. Oh, I'm in the alley, 'cause I don't get good reception in my apartment. The noise you hear is just some kids playing ball. Yes, I know, but I can't take the Friday off. I can pick you up after I get off work and we could leave then, I guess." She tried to see the man's face as he paced back and forth, but he was wearing a baseball cap and she couldn't see his features at all. "Alright then, Ted, I will be at your place around nine. We will just drive straight through. Did you get reservations? Great! Okay then, see you tomorrow night." She watched him put the phone in his pocket. Then he entered the apartment across from hers. She saw the lights go on as he entered each room. She heard the kids playing baseball in the street. She saw the truck coming down the narrow alley and in fear for the children's safety, she gulped for air, but the boys moved out of the street, as the truck's horn blared. She leaned in towards the window and her eyes were right above the sill. She realized she could see down the whole street. She glanced at the apartment across from her. There was the man, his back was to her, but he was moving about in his kitchen. She saw him open his refrigerator, then he turned toward her. She ducked down out of fear that he saw her watching, but her room was dark and there was no way he could see her. It seemed to her as if he was looking right at her. He paused and stood motionless, a wooden spoon and a stainless steel bowl were held   in his hands, as he stared out the window.

She moved away from the window.

But the next morning, she found herself on her knees with both hands on the window sill, waiting for the man to emerge from his apartment. He came out the door and she watched as he locked his apartment door. He pushed a button on his cell phone and began talking. "Damn! I hate having to walk outside to use this stupid phone. Yeah, I'm on my way to work. Yeah, it's a crap job, but once I finish my night courses and have my degree I can find a good job. Well, no, I hadn't thought of that." He laughed. "Okay, well, I'd better get crackin' and get to work. Talk later, yeah."

He pushed a button and then shoved the phone into his pocket. He began to walk down the street. His hand brushed her window sill as he walked past her window. She sat very still. She could smell his masculine cologne wafting through the one- inch crack. It lingered in her nose for several seconds as she watched him until he rounded the corner at the end of the alley.

Chapter 2

She heard a knock at the front door. She looked through the small peep hole and saw her Aunt Mahibah. She was holding a casserole pot in her two hands out in front of her. "Inayah, it's me, Aunt Mahibah. Open the door."

Inayah unlocked the two locks on the door to let her aunt inside. "It is so good to see you!" She exclaimed in earnest as she kissed her aunt's cold cheeks. The weather had just recently turned into a crisp cool fall. There had been slight snow flurries.

"Oh, it's getting cold. Perfect weather for this, I have brought some Bahmieh. You will eat it and become strong." She didn't even pause before she added, as if it were an everyday occurrence, "I heard from your father that he has arranged a marriage for you with the landlord." She paused thoughtfully, "Though in truth, if you are too strong for the old man, the old goat will surely die!" She chuckled. "He is 64 and shouldn't have his eyes on such a young bride, at least not in America."

Mahibah almost choked. "My father arranged my marriage? He did not tell me anything about it."

"Of course not. He knows that you will not be happy with the news. What woman is happy with such news? I remember my own misfortune. Now, my husband is a bald, toothless, bony man who sits all day in front of the TV, even though he hasn't learned a word of English. He is useless." She shook her head, "But you, oh my love, you are beautiful and young and you don't deserve such a fate. The landlord has a terrible temper and I fear he would beat you daily."

Inayah moaned, "Oh, what have I done to deserve such a fate? Why would my father do such a thing"?

Her aunt shook her head, "Your father is desperate for money. The Americans give him a low salary and he wants more than this. Having his son-in-law as the landlord will be advantageous for him. The man is from the same region as you are. To your father this is a match made in heaven."

Inayah stared stupefied at her aunt, then as if someone had poked her with a sharp pin she said, "Oh how terrible of me. Let me take that." Her niece reached out and took the pot from her aunt's hands. "Thank you for the lamb stew. How ungrateful of me. Please, sit down." She took the pot into the kitchen and returned quickly. As she walked back into the living room she asked, "When is this marriage to be?"

Her Aunt shook her head. "Sadly, soon."

"Oh my God, how can this be! I don't want to be married. If my father is tired of caring for me, I can leave his home, but to marry me to some old man is the worst travesty I can even imagine."

"The old landlord paid a lot for you. There was a large exchange of money, as well as free rent here in the apartments." The Aunt crossed her legs, "But we must not let it happen."

"How can we not? Oh Aunt, I am truly doomed."

Her aunt shook her head. "You are not doomed. You are young and you have many years of youth still ahead of you. We will think of a solution." She lowered her voice to almost a whisper, "I will not let this happen to you."

Inayah sat very still as she thought. Then she leaned closer to her aunt, "May I confide in you, Aunt Mahibah?" Inayah rested her fingertips on her aunt's arm.

"Always, my child." The aunt looked into her niece's bright eyes.

"There is this young man. He stands outside my window and speaks on his cellphone. He seems like a good person and..."

"I know this man. Yes, he is a good person. He is the janitor in the store on the corner of the next street. Sometimes he runs the cash register. Yes, a very handsome young man." Her aunt reached out and hugged her. "Yes, you should go and see this young man."

"Go see him? But he is not from our culture. He would not even consider a woman in a niqab." Her fingers pulled up on her long dress.

"I will get you some American clothes to wear when you go to see him. You must go." She hugged her niece again. "I must spare you the same fate as I have had. Mine has been a sad, lonely life. You deserve much more. Your mother would have wanted you to have more. You are in America now. Things are different here." The aunt stood up. "So I need to go now to go to the store to buy you some decent American clothes."

"But father will be furious."

"Your father must not know, Inayah. This is not something that will please him." Her aunt walked to the front door. "Lock these behind me." She said as she pointed to the locks and opened the door and left without another word.

Inayah leaned her back against the door and whispered, "Marriage. Oh please God, no!" Her thoughts raced. *Should I run away? Should I kill the landlord?* Then, almost immediately she thought how absurd that would be.

A day later she once again heard the insistent knock on the door. When she peeked through the peep hole and saw her aunt, she immediately opened the door. Her aunt was carrying a large bag. "I have bought you some clothes." As she spoke she reached into the bag and pulled each item out. "Some jeans," she pulled out a pair of nice denim jeans, "And a nice blouse and some lovely underwear. You can go out to see the young man. His name is James. I asked him his name when I went to the store. He was sweeping and I accidently bumped into him," her aunt smiled broadly, "I said excuse me and then I said, 'and what's your name young man?' and he told me. Oh, Inayah, he seems like such a good man."

Inayah was speechless. "You bumped into him? You spoke with him?"

Her aunt's smile became even broader, "I did. I really like his very blue eyes. You would have such beautiful babies with this man." She laughed and Inayah's cheeks became pink.

"Aunt Mahibah, what you are asking me to do is very dangerous. If my father should find out, he would kill me."

Mahibah nodded, "By the time he finds out you will be married to James and he must accept it. You worry too much, dear niece."

Inayah rolled what Mahibah was saying into the memory drawers of her mind. Hadn't Mahibah's sister been murdered by her uncle and her father years ago? Hadn't the two men chopped off her young aunt's head when they found her with a man sitting on a bench by the harbor? "Aunt Mahibah, you are asking me to go against everything we believe in, to expose myself to this man without my niqab and to encourage him." She stopped speaking.

Her aunt leaned in very close to her, "If I had the chance years ago I would have taken it without thinking for a moment. I am telling you, my dear sweet Inayah, you do not want a lifetime of submitting yourself to an unhappy torturous life. In the beginning my husband beat me, now he is too old and he knows that I would kill him if he tried." Her voice sounded as if it turned into the murderous rattle of a snake as she spoke. "I don't want this life for you. I want more for you. I want what your mother would have wanted for you." She wanted to add, *I want this for all Arabic women,* but thought better of it. This was not about political change; this was not about Arab women's rights. Yet, Mahibah knew that it truly was just that. One woman at a time would find freedom. Now, it was Inayah's turn to fly.

"You must do this, Inayah. Go to see the man, James."

Inayah reached out and took the lace bra and panties from her aunt's hands. "I am to wear these?" She held the panties with the black lace triangle that she knew would only cover her private space, leaving her backside totally bare. "Women wear these?" She asked as she pulled on the elastic. Her aunt nodded.

When Mahibah dug into the bag and withdrew a small colorful plastic bag, she smiled. "This is make- up. You might have to practice, but there is pink lipstick and eyeliner and a wand for making your lashes longer and cream and soft pink for your pale cheeks." Then, as if it was more important than any of the other things which her aunt had purchased, Mahibah withdrew a large bottle of cream. "And this is to remove it all so that there will be no trace of it on your face, especially your eyes." She knew that Inayah's eyes would be the one thing that would always be open for inspection by her father.

"Aunt, how do you know about all these things?"

The older woman laughed, "I buy magazines."

Later, after her aunt had said her good byes, Inayah went to the bathroom to try on her new American clothes. She marveled at how snuggly the jeans fit her, as if her aunt had measured her body for a custom fit. The white blouse revealed her swan-like neck and accentuated her tiny waist, which was always camouflaged in layers of the material of her niqab. She began to apply the make up her aunt had bought for her.

She stared at herself, wondering if she would be perceived as beautiful, or if James would find her offensive like he found the woman with the fish lips? She quickly removed the blouse and pants, as she stood in front of the mirror. She briefly admired the lace triangle covering her private parts. Her breasts were gently concealed in black lace cups. Her flat stomach contracted. Then, in a frenzy she abruptly ripped the panties off and slid them down her legs. In moments she had replaced her new clothes with the psychological comfort of the niqab. *How will I ever leave the house dressed like that?* She asked herself. "Not only will I leave, I must leave." She said bravely.

She hid her new clothes under her bed, hoping that her father would never think to look there for anything. She then went to sit on the floor to look out the window. She didn't bother to push the sheer curtain aside, but watched through the curtain as the world outside passed by. The children were on their way home from school. They were laughing and tossing a ball back and forth as they walked. The mailman went from door to door, sliding letters through the slits in the doors. Then, she saw him. James was walking towards his front door. He had his cell phone up against his ear. She put her ear in the one-inch gap, listening intently for his voice.

"Listen, I can't help it if my boss wants me to work Saturday. You'll have to just go without me. Yeah, it's a bummer. No, I don't want to date her again. I don't know. There was something about her that I just couldn't get into. Maybe it was her red lipstick. Her lips looked like they were going to reach out and swallow my head." He laughed, his warm deep laugh. "Okay, I'll catch ya later."

She watched as he slid the phone into his pocket and bounded into his house. It was daylight so she couldn't see into his windows. She wondered why he had come home so early from work. She wondered who the girl with the red lips was in his life. She made a mental note that he would be working on Saturday. Fortunately, her father also worked on Saturdays. She formulated her plan. *I will do this,* she thought. *I will do it because I must, because to not do it will surely mean my death. I would will myself to die before I will marry the despicable landlord. All I have to do is wait until my father leaves the house. Then I will dress and I will leave.* She thought about it for a moment, then she changed her mind. *No, I will carry my clothes in a bag to my aunt's house. I will dress in her bathroom and leave from there. I think that is a better plan.* She thought deeply again and felt her heart pounding in her chest, *Or should I just dress here and not involve my aunt?* She chewed on her thumb, nervously. *Okay, I will dress here. I don't want to involve her.* Then, as if it solidified her plans, she said aloud, "Okay, yes, that is what I must do."

Saturday was a crisp sunny day. She watched James leave for work. As usual, he had his cell phone pushed against his ear. He paused right outside her bedroom window. She could hear him talking as if he was in her room talking right to her. "Well, you guys have fun. I'm glad you got someone to go with you. It's a great day for hitting jackpots!" He chuckled. "Swig a few for me, would you? Nope. I have a long day. I'm on the cash register today, that's why I had to work. He is short people. Yeah, bummer is right. Okay dude. Have fun!" He pushed his cell phone buttons and then plopped the phone in his jean's pocket. She put up her hand as if she was going to reach out and touch him, but of course, she wouldn't. She couldn't anyhow because the window was only open its usual inch. If it was open far enough, she could have reached out and touched his leg.   She watched his back as he walked away from her. Today would be different. Today she would go to the store and talk with him, face to face. Today all barriers would come down.

She was self-conscious while walking down the street. She had pinned her hair up in a French twist, so it did not flow behind her. For the most part she kept her head down and her eyes barely looking at the area in front of her. She strode quickly, seeing the cracks in the sidewalk coming into view and then disappearing behind her. There was the store. She had been there once before while dressed in her niqab, but here she was with her face decorated with make- up and the feminine top and tight fitting jeans. She had rehearsed her lines that she would say to him. She pushed open the store door and there James was, with a broom in his hand, sweeping the entry.

"Well, hello there!" He said as soon as he saw her. "I haven't seen you in here before."

She found her voice locked deep within her chest, "Oh, but I have been in before." She answered.

"Oh listen, honey, I would have known if I saw you before. You're beautiful." He was straight forward.

She stammered, "I, uh, I'm just here for some yogurt."

"It's in the back refrigerator section." He watched as she went down the aisle. He thought, *Wow, she has a beautiful backside, too.* When she placed the yogurt on the counter his hand touched hers briefly. She felt his warmth tingle in her fingers. "So what's your name?" He smiled.

"Inayah." She answered quickly, but immediately wished she had given him an American name like Susie or Mary instead.

"That's Arabic, isn't it?" He snapped the cash drawer shut.

She nodded.

"Do you live around here?" His questions were non-ending.

"Yes, I do." She watched as he carefully placed her yogurt in a bag.

His blue eyes locked on her golden brown eyes. Neither of them looked away. The magnetic pull was so great that both of them felt that to look away would diminish the energy flowing between them.

He was confused by the intensity of these brief moments. "Do you date?" He asked.

She did not answer at first, but then whispered, "I haven't."

"Ah, but would you?" Still, his eyes did not release hers.

"I don't know. Perhaps." She felt a stirring deep within her, a feeling that she could not quite identify or name. She had never felt like this before.

He whispered, "Like would you date someone like me?"

She grabbed for the bag, "I can't right now." Yet her eyes continued to stare into his. Neither of them disengaged.

"Are you engaged or something?" It seemed that he wouldn't let go of the bag and held it with one hand as she also held it.

"Or something." She answered. Then, in a very brave moment she said, "My father has found a husband for me. The husband is an old man and he wants a young bride like me."

He clenched the bag harder, "An arranged marriage? We don't do those things in America! Do you want to marry him?"

She shook her head and some of her hair fell out of the French twist, in one long spiraling lock of honey brown hair, onto her shoulder. "No, I don't even know this man. I haven't even seen him." At last he blinked and they both looked away, the mesmerizing trance was gone.

He continued to hold onto the bag which held the yogurt. "Well, let me tell you something, honey, you should go out with me and then we will see if you want to marry that old dude." He looped his pinkie finger over hers and then he released the bag. She clutched it to her body. He asked, "Will you go out with me?"

"I-I don't know." She stuttered again.

"Can we meet somewhere; would that be better?" He was persistent. "Can I call you?"

"I don't have a phone."

"There's a store around the corner. You can buy a cellphone. Do you have money for a cellphone?"

She looked down.

"Here." He reached into his pocket and took out his wallet. "Here's forty dollars. I'd happily give you more, but you would have to wait for my payday. It should buy you a cheap phone and some minutes. Come back through here to give me your number so that I can call you."

She didn't take the money which he was waving in the air. "I can't." She said as she turned to go out the door.

"Inayah, please. I want you to get a phone so that you can call me, then. I promise I won't call you, but if you need me you can call me."

She turned to look at him. He had very blue eyes and ash-blond curly hair. He looked so sincere, as he begged her to call him. He continued, "Please take the money. I want you to have a phone."

She shook her head, "You haven't even told me your name."

"James. My name is James."

"I can't take money from you, James. My culture--you don't understand how serious this is."

He lowered his voice in his attempt to control her response, "Take the money."

She grabbed at the cash and ran out the door. She turned left, away from her house, on her way to the cellphone store. Self-consciously she picked up a phone. It was only nineteen ninety- five and then she would have enough money left over to buy a card for phone minutes. The man at the counter stared at her for some time. "Don't I know you from somewhere?" He asked. He was an Arab, she could tell that much from his face, but she couldn't remember if she had seen him before. She shook her head.

"So you like that phone? Okay, but there is another one for a little bit more and it is superior to that one."

She didn't speak, but put the phone on the counter. She also put the money on the counter and took a phone card off of the display shelf. "I will take these." She announced.

He began to punch at the cash register keys. "Are you sure I don't know you? You just seem so familiar?" She shook her head, but she racked her brain trying to remember where she had seen this man before.

"Okay, there you go. Do you know how to activate the phone?"

She nodded and went out the door before he could ask another question. After she had walked half way back, she stood on a corner and activated the phone with the card minutes. She took note of her phone number. As she walked toward James' market she felt her steps become quicker. She hurried in the door and saw him at the cash register helping an old lady put her groceries into a portable cart. James saw her enter, but he didn't say a word. He watched her get in line behind the lady. Once they were alone, she said, "Here's my number, do you have a pen?"

He gave her a pen and a cash register receipt to write on. She wrote her number and then turned to leave. "Wait, Inayah, when will I see you again? Will you call me? Here is my number." He wrote his number on a cash register receipt. He handed it to her and touched her fingers with his. For a few moments neither of them moved their hands. They just left their hands suspended in the air, lightly touching. He whispered, "I must see you again. Please?"

She nodded and left the store.

For some reason she tasted the bile of fear in her throat. She began to run down the street until her breath was fast and labored. She fumbled with her key and finally, mercifully, the door opened. She banged it behind her and latched the two locks. She ran into her room and shut the door. She pulled off her blouse and shimmied out of her jeans. She yanked at her panties and bra. She rolled them all into a ball and shoved them under her bed. She slid into her niqab. Then panic seized her when she realized she had forgotten to remove her make up! She ran into the bathroom with the jar of make-up remover in her hand. She locked the door and quickly removed her niqab. She hung it on the hook behind the door and looked into the mirror. Her beautiful golden brown eyes were rimmed in a soft black line, her lashes rich and long, her lips a soft luscious pink. She smeared the make-up remover cream all over her face, rolling her fingertips in circles removing all signs of the make up from her eyes and mouth. When she was sure that there wasn't a speck of pink or black or brow pencil remaining on her face, she splashed cold water on her face. She took a towel and patted her face dry. She pulled the niqab off the hook and draped it over her head. Her eyes looked at her mirror image from behind the darkness.

She thought, *I will never be the same. The girl I see with those eyes does not exist anymore.* She reached out and put her palm against the glass image of herself. "She is gone," she whispered. She heard the bang of the front door. Her father was home. Her air sucked into her chest. *Will he know that the girl is gone?* She asked herself. Fear poured into every inch of her body.

When she came out to face him, he had his nose deep into the Arabic newspaper he had brought home with him. He didn't even pull it down to look at her when she said, "Hello father." He had grunted. She went into the kitchen to prepare his supper.

Chapter 3

Veiled by the opaque curtain, she watched James come home from work, as she sat in her place by the window. She put her nose near the crack and tried to smell his scent as he walked by. She saw him unlock his door and go into his apartment. The light went on in his kitchen. She saw him pull things out of his refrigerator and set them on his counter. She silently wished that she could prepare his dinner for him. She imagined how he would come home to her and hug her tightly and kiss her.

The next morning, she was right back at her post; she had fallen asleep on the floor and woke up to watch him again. He was once again leaving for work. As usual he was speaking on his cellphone. She pulled the curtain aside and put her ear close the window crack. She could hear him clearly. "Let me tell you, Joe, this is one gorgeous gal. I don't know. She lives somewhere near me. You should see her eyes; they are the most beautiful golden brown eyes with maybe flecks of green in them. No, we didn't. I wish we had. She's gorgeous. Her butt just fills out her jeans as if they were sewed on her. No, she said she would call me. I know, I know, but I promised her I wouldn't call her. Heck I don't know. Maybe she will never let me see her again. She's special, Joe. I know that much. It's like I hit the friggin' jack pot. Oh, speaking of which, did you hit a lot of jackpots over the weekend? Well, you know the house always wins. Yeah, okay, I will talk to you after work. I'm on my way now." He hung up the phone just as he brushed her window sill with his leg.

She sighed. If I wanted, I could have just touched him. She thought. It would have been so easy. Or I could have called out his name and he would have turned right at my window to look at me. Then, he would know. He would know where I am and he would come and save me. But she didn't touch him and she didn't call out his name. He walked right past her window and he never looked in. Even if he had the opaque curtain would have blocked his view. He would not have known that she was inside.

Finally, days later, she called him. His phone rang three times. Then she heard his voice. She hung up. Within seconds her phone rang. "Inayah? Why did you hang up?" he whispered softly.

"I was afraid." She answered.

"When can I see you again?" he asked. "Can you come to the store today?"

"Yes."

"Come now," he urged.

"Okay." She whispered.

When he saw her jeans and the same blouse, thoughts crossed his mind. *She's poor. She has nothing else to wear.* Her cheeks turned crimson when she saw him looking so intensely at her clothes. Her aunt hadn't thought about that. Every time he saw her she would have to be in the same blouse and the same pants. The blouse was slightly wrinkled from being rolled up into a ball under her bed.

"Let me get someone to cover for me and we can go somewhere." He left her standing in the foyer and he went to the back of the store. She stood to the side of the door as people came in. He returned quickly, "Sorry about that. I got Robert to cover for me. I told him we won't be long, but I just have to see you away from the store." He linked his arm through hers and walked her out of the store. He led her down the street and turned right and then right again until they were nearing a great expanse of green lawn with swings and slides for children. "We can sit on a bench a talk here in the park."

She glanced at the children playing on the swings and sitting in the sand with their shovels and pails.

"Inayah, why didn't you call me sooner?" He draped his arm around her shoulders as they walked to a bench.

"I didn't know if I should."

He laughed, "Of course you should! I was worried, you know. I didn't know if you got carried away in a sack to be married to that guy." His smile faded from his face. "I was really concerned, but I promised not to call you and a promise is a promise."

She folded her hands in her lap. She could feel his fingers lightly moving on her shoulder. "I shouldn't be here." She began to stand up, but he pressed his fingers against her shoulder.

"No, don't go. What are you afraid of?" With his free hand he turned her face towards him. "I won't bite, you know." He grinned. "What's wrong with getting to know each other better? We could go to the movies or how 'bout we have dinner together?"

She shook her head violently back and forth, "No, I can't. You don't understand."

He gently placed his index finger under her chin and lifted her head, "I DO understand. What you don't understand, Inayah, is that you are free here in America. No one can tell you who you have to marry or what to do. You are not a child."

"My father..." she began, but he put his finger to her lips.

"Shh. Your father has no control over you. You are an adult woman." He leaned towards her and she could feel his breath against her lips and then she felt his mouth close on hers. At first she was totally alarmed, she pushed her hands against his chest in protest, but he didn't move and continued to kiss her lips. Her tense body relaxed, as he put his arms tightly around her and pulled her close. "Inayah, beautiful Inayah, you have nothing to worry about. Nothing at all, my sweet Inayah."

Her head felt as though her mind had floated out of the top of it and was drifting in clouds somewhere high above her. She was intoxicated by his musky scent and found herself leaning into his body, not wanting the kiss to end. "Inayah, will you go with me to dinner tonight?" He asked.

As if she was a horse stung by a biting fly, she jumped up and off the bench. "No! I can't. I need to go home now. I shouldn't have met you like this." Her voice was frantic. He stood up quickly and wrapped her in his arms again.

"Dearest Inayah, you have nothing to worry about. I will never hurt you."

"No, you don't understand. My father, I, you don't know, I just can't, that's all."

He ran his hand over her hair, disturbing the tight French twist. Her golden brown hair tumbled down to below her waist. He gasped. "I'm sorry, I didn't mean to do that. Oh, your hair is so beautiful!"

She quickly grabbed at her hair and rolled it tightly and pinned it back onto her head.

"Oh sweetie, you don't have to be embarrassed, your hair is lovely, you should always leave it down. I want to run my fingers through it. I want to kiss you and hold you and never let you go." He leaned towards her and kissed her again.

"James, you just can't know. We are in danger. I am in danger."

He yanked her closer to his body, "No one will ever hurt you. Believe me."

She saw the flash of light in his blue eyes and she knew he meant what he was saying, but then, he didn't know her father. He didn't know that her father had already been an accomplice in the murder of her aunt. He was capable of anything. He was ruthless and honor was his main virtue in life. "I must go now." She whispered. She could still feel his kiss against her lips. She took a gulp of the crisp fall air. "You don't understand, James. You just don't. We can't see each other again." She turned her back and began to walk away. She heard him call out her name, but she didn't turn around. Then she heard him running behind her. He pulled on her shoulder and whipped her around to face him.

"No, I won't let you do this, Inayah. I have been with many girls. Tons of girls, but I have never felt like this. Ever! I am not going to let you go." He kissed her forehead, her cheek and then her other cheek. She closed her eyes and then he kissed one closed eyelid and then the other. Then, as gently as a feather brushing against them, he kissed her lips. He pulled back and whispered, "We will figure this out. I promise we will."

"I have to go."

"Call me. You promise to call me?" he asked.

She nodded and turned away from him, walking as fast as she could.

She hadn't gone far when she thought she heard him walking behind her. She turned and saw the shopkeeper from the cellphone shop. He shouted, "I know who you are!" He was smiling. "You are Mohammed's daughter. I recognize your voice and those eyes I would know anywhere."

She turned to look at him. "You must be mistaken." She said.

"Oh no. I know you. Your father brought you with him when you first came to this country. He bought a very expensive cellphone." The man was right, of course, her father had been in the shop with her when they first arrived and he had purchased the most expensive cellphone in the shop. "You ARE Mohammed's daughter. I just didn't recognize you without your niqab." His eyes scanned her body, up and down and then up and down again, lingering on her breasts for some time before he added, "You are quite a beauty in your western clothes."

She thought that she saw drips of saliva on the corners of the man's mouth. "A man like me might want to marry a girl like you." He grinned. "I am quite well to do with my own cellphone shop."

Foolishly she said, "I'm promised."

His eyebrows raised, "Oh?   Well that is unfortunate, isn't it?"

"I have to go now." She turned and began to hurry down the street. She quickly unlocked her door and repeated the routine of removing her make- up and putting on her niqab, but she did not go into the kitchen to prepare dinner, nor did she sit by the window. Dusk dimmed the light in the apartment. She opened the front door and hurried down the street. She heard the wind flapping her niqab behind her as she walked.

He was standing behind the counter. His hands were putting items in a bag. He murmured something about a discount on Saturdays and then he took the man's money and put it into the cash register. The man bumped past her and then, he looked up and saw her standing there. A huge smile lit up his face in anticipation. "It's you," he exclaimed.

"Yes, it's me. I thought I should come back." She whispered.

"Well, good. I was hoping you would, but I am surprised you are out when it is getting dark." He added.

"Yes, well, it is important. Will you walk with me?" She asked.

"Of course. I will meet you out front after I lock up the store. It won't take long."

She nodded and stepped outside the store and waited with her back to the door. It wasn't long before she felt his hand through her arm and he began to guide her down the street. "You look so different in your niqab." He said as he hurried along. "Where would you like to go?"

"Can we go to your apartment?" She asked.

He squeezed her elbow tightly, "Of course!" After going left and then left and then right and then right, they came to an old brownstone house. "This is my house. I don't live in an apartment." He quickly unlocked the door and she pushed past him into the large living room.

He ignored her for a few moments as he lit the fireplace and threw a log on the gas burning fire. "It's getting so cold already." He said as he stoked the fire. She watched him with mild curiosity. Then he fell onto the couch and patted the seat next to him. "Come sit. Sit right here, next to me." She plopped down next to him. He put his arm around her and fondled her shoulder. "Isn't this cozy?" He asked.

"Yes, very cozy." She repeated. Then, in one swift movement she withdrew the knife from her boot. She leaned over him and in one swift movement slit his throat from one ear to the other. She felt the knife stop and then shoved it harder until his head was completely severed. She threw the macabre head, with its eyes wide and its mouth in a permanent scream into the fire. She heard it pop and sizzle and she could smell burning hair and flesh. She wiped her knife on the fabric of the couch and then made her way to a backdoor off of the kitchen. She rushed down the streets towards her apartment.

She fumbled with her keys and then finally was able to unlock the door. She went straight to her dark room and sat down by the windowsill. James' lights were on. She put her chin on the windowsill, sniffing at the air from the outside. Two people walked by her window. She didn't move. She watched James in his kitchen. He was pouring liquid from a carton into a glass. She watched as he drank it, tilting his head back, exposing his white neck to her.

Her father did not come home that night. She never left her perch at the window. When morning came she heard James' voice. He was standing next to her window with his hand on the exterior sill. She could smell his cologne on his fingers. She reached out and touched his fingers, lightly, ever so lightly. He removed his hand and flapped at the air, thinking that the crawling feeling on his knuckles was an annoying fly. He placed his hand back on the sill while he continued to talk on his phone. She touched his knuckles again with the tip of her finger. Again, he pulled his hand away and wildly flapped at the air. "Okay, listen, Joe, I just can't. Yes, it's the girl. I'm seeing her. Yes, she and I went to the park. I know, I know, but she's different. Okay, I say that a lot, but this time I mean it. She's special. I don't know what it is about her, but I want to spend every moment with her. She's so delicate and so sweet and so pure. Okay, yes, yes, maybe. Maybe I'm falling in love, but when you meet her you are going to want to steal her from me, I can tell you that!" He laughed. Inayah put her nose into the window crack and sniffed. Oh, she wanted his lips on hers. She could smell his cologne. She reached out and touched his knuckles one more time, but this time he turned away and started down the street. The last words she heard were, "Okay. I'm going to ask her to my place for dinner or lunch or breakfast." He laughed, "Well, a man can hope, can't he?" He trailed off down the street on his way to work. She stayed there watching as the children walked to school. She saw the mailman come purposefully striding down the street. She turned away from the window and let the curtain fall into its natural place.

The tapping on the door drew her out of her room. She looked through the peephole and saw her Aunt Mahibah. She opened the door hastily. "Aunt, how are you?"

Her aunt hugged her, "Are you alright, Inayah?"

"Yes, I'm fine. What's the matter?"

"Oh, thank God. There's been a murder, right down the street. A business owner had his head cut off. It has to be a revenge murder. They cut off his entire head and threw it into the fire."

Inayah gasped, "Into the fire?"

"Yes! Can you imagine? Such a ruthless, brutal murder. I know the man. He is from our country. Perhaps he was mixed up with the mob or something. It's horrific, reminds me of the days back home." She patted Inayah's back, "So glad you are safe, my dear. I was so worried."

"I am fine."

"Have you seen, James?"

Inayah nodded. "Several times."

Her aunt let out a surprised, "Oh."

"Yes, he wants to take me to dinner, which of course is impossible."

Her aunt put her finger on her chin, "Not totally impossible. You could tell your father you are coming to my house for dinner."

"But Aunt Mahibah, why would I go there for dinner?"

"Because I want you to. Since women do not eat with men, he wouldn't expect me to ask him." She grinned. "And they think THEY are the smart ones." She chuckled. "Then you could sneak off to have dinner with James."

"But Aunt Mahibah, aren't you forgetting a very important thing?   James lives right over there." She pointed towards James' apartment. "It isn't as if it is safe to just come and go. I would have to wear my American clothes and change and, it is just too complicated."

Her Aunt sat very quietly for a long moment. "True. Nothing worth having is easy. While I think some more, tell me all about him."

"He's wonderful. He's kind and sweet and gentle and protective and--"

"My, my, my. You have fallen in love."

Inayah's eyes met her aunt's eyes. "I suppose I have. But aunt Mahibah, this love is impossible. I am so embarrassed. I have gone alone to see a man, who has seen me without my niqab. I have defiled myself. This romance can never be."

Mahibah shook her head, "Nonsense, it can and will be. We will wait until your father goes to pray at the mosque. This will give you enough time to meet with James. You could go to a restaurant." She paused, "Or to a hotel far from here."

"You are crazy." She looked at her aunt with shock. "My father will kill me."

Her aunt was silent. She knew her niece was right. If her father found out about any secret rendezvous, he would surely kill her. "He will not find out." Her aunt said with conviction.

The two of them planned, talking out each part and revising it, until they knew the plan was perfect. When her aunt put her hand on the doorknob to leave, she smiled, "Do not worry, Inayah. Our plan is flawless, simply and perfectly flawless."

Inayah was not so sure.

Chapter 4

Mahibah smiled broadly as she took the pink flowered dress out of the bag. "You have to wear something else besides jeans."

"Oh, it's beautiful! Aunt Mahibah, you shouldn't have!" Inayah's eyes opened wide. She reached out and slid her fingers along the material. "Oh, I love it."

"And here are some nylons and," she paused, "shoes." She lifted a pair of black pumps out of the bag. "Now you will look like a real woman in a dress." She announced with satisfaction. "Tonight you can surprise James. We will tell your father that you are having dinner with me."

Mahibah released the dress into Inayah's hands. The young girl caressed the material with her fingertips. "I have never seen anything so beautiful. I don't know how to thank you."

"There is no need for thank you. I just wish I could see you all dressed and ready to go."

"I will dress at your house, Aunt Mahibah." The young woman smiled. "I can't believe it; I feel like a fairy princess."

"Now I must go and talk to James," her aunt grinned. "He must know that you cannot go to his house across the street. It is too risky for you. Your father might see you. He must be discrete. I know that now you must hide and it seems that you are so deceitful, but believe me, it will not always be this way."

Mahibah hurried down the street towards the store. She knew that James would be working. Her niqab whipped around her legs as she walked. She wondered what he would think of Inayah's aunt dressed in Arabic clothes? Would he immediately be turned off by her appearance and not even talk to her? James was at the cash register. He looked up when he saw her enter the store, "Welcome." He said automatically, like he did with everyone who entered the store. She rambled down an aisle, waiting for the line to dissipate long enough for her to go to talk to him without other ears tuned in and listening.

"James," she said his name as her fingers curled like a claw around his wrist. "You don't know me, but I am Inayah's aunt, Mahibah."

He didn't pull his hand away, but smiled at her, "Yes, how are you?"

"I have a message for you. Inayah wants to meet you tonight, here at the store at five, and then you must take her away from here for dinner. Far away." Her eyes stared into his. "She cannot meet and go to your apartment." Then she pressed her lips together and said no more.

He nodded, "Okay, if that's what she wants, then I will meet her here. Where is she now?"

Mahibah turned to leave, releasing his wrist abruptly. He knew better than to call her back. He watched her leave and saw her turn right, headed back from where she had come. His thoughts began to tip toe into his brief moments with Inayah. He longed to kiss her soft lips again, to feel her soft skin beneath his fingertips. He could barely concentrate for the rest of the day. He made several mistakes on the cash register. He had to redo the orders. The minutes crawled by as he waited for five o'clock.

Inayah looked into the large mirror in her aunt's bathroom. Her aunt had a much nicer apartment than theirs, but then, she had been there many years and added her own touches. The mirror was huge, with bright tulip-shaped lights above it. She could see her face quite clearly as she put on her make-up. She didn't smear it on, but took her time outlining her eyes and adding just the right amount of blush. Then she sat on the toilet to put on the nylons. Her aunt had told her how to bunch up the leg all the way to the toe and then she put the nylon on the tip of her toes. She pulled it up her leg and then she did the same with her other leg. She stood and pulled the rest of the pantyhose up over her tiny hips, jiggly her hips side to side. She put her dress over her head and stretched her arms into the sleeves. "Wow." She said aloud as she stared at herself in the mirror.

She brushed her long hair and began to twirl it on top of her head, securing it with several pins. She was ready. When she left her niqab on the bronze hook in the small closet, she left her old self behind.

Her aunt handed her a black knit sweater. "You may need this to stay warm."

Inayah took the sweater and placed it over her arm. Her aunt reached out and hugged her tightly. She didn't release her hold for some time. Then, her aunt pushed her away from her with both hands and said, "You look like your mother. You are so lovely."

Inayah's eyes looked down, "I miss her. I wish she were here to give me advice and support, but I am so grateful to have you Aunt Mahibah."

Her aunt nodded, "I miss her, too. You would think I would have intense love for my own brother, but it is your mother who I loved. She was such a good woman." She shook her head, "It is terrible the times we live in." Then she reached into a pocket and brought out a wad of money. "Take this. A woman should never be in the streets without some money. You may need a cab or you may need something."

"But..." Inayah protested as her aunt closed her fingers with the money in her fist.

"Shh. Now go. I will cover for you tonight. You have no worries. Enjoy yourself. Be happy, Inayah. James is a good man. Be happy together."

Inayah went out into the street and felt the cool breeze against her legs. She was glad that she had the nylons to keep her legs somewhat warm. She grabbed the edges of the sweater and held tightly to keep it closed in front of her. Her heels clacked on the cement as she hurried. She didn't look into the eyes of passing people, but kept her eyes straight ahead. She went into the store and searched for James, but he was nowhere to be seen. Another man was working at the cash register. She wanted to ask him if he had seen James, but her voice would not come out. She stood by the front door and then decided to go outside to wait. Five minutes passed and still she did not see James. She kept looking up and down the street, but he was nowhere to be seen. She felt an arm around her waist and turned around to look into his eyes. "James!"

"Who'd you expect, the Easter bunny?" He kissed her mouth.

"Oh James, not here in front of the store in public." She cast her eyes downwards.

"Come on! Your chariot awaits!" He took her hand and led her to a grey car. He popped open the door and she got into the passenger seat. He hurried around to the driver's seat and got in. "We are getting out of here." He turned on the key and then punched at the gas. She felt her head jerk back against the seat. He reached over and took her hand. "I love your dress."

"Thank you."

"I love everything about you," he glanced at her and then kept his eyes on the road ahead. Before long they had driven out of the city and were headed into the country. "There's this place I know you are going to love. It's way out in Manassas. But I got us reservations for dinner." The car swerved into a turn and she leaned into his shoulder and then flipped back towards her own window. "Sorry about that." He chuckled. "I have a bit of Mario Andretti in me, I think." He laughed again. Finally, after over an hour, the car stopped and he ran around to open her door. "Here we are. Do you like it?" She saw an old barn that had been converted into a restaurant. Around the sides and the back were little cottages. "Have I told you that you are beautiful?" He kissed her cheek. Her cheeks became hot and pink at the touch of his lips.

Once inside they were greeted by a hostess in a gingham blue checked dress and white crisp apron. "Welcome. Do you have a reservation?"

"Yes, James Calahan for two for dinner." He squeezed Inayah's hand.

"Yes, right this way." The hostess led them to a corner booth that almost seemed like a little private room with enclosed walls on three sides.

He helped Inayah slide in and then he slid in beside her.

"The menu." The hostess handed each of them a menu, but they both let it fall to the tablecloth. "May I get you a drink? Wine, beer, a mixed drink?"

"We will have a glass of your house red wine, please." He nodded to the waitress. She smiled politely and then left them alone.

"James, I don't drink." Inayah protested.

"Today you will have your first glass of wine to toast our future." He smiled and kissed her lips. She felt like she was already intoxicated.

"But..."

"Hush." He put his finger to her lips. "Tonight is special. Very, very special."

The hostess brought two long stemmed wine glasses. She filled them to the brim. James lifted his glass and sniffed and then he sipped. "Wonderful." He nodded to the hostess.

"Good. The waitress will be here shortly to take your orders."

James turned to Inayah. "Lift your glass sweetheart. This is our toast."

She lifted her glass and he clinked it with his. "To us, may we be together forever even into eternity." He sipped and then she sipped.

The room began to spin by the time she was on her fifth sip. "James, I am so dizzy."

He smiled, "Wine can do that. After you eat you will feel better. What would you like?" He opened one of the menus and read some of the selections.

"Whatever you have, I will have." She stated politely.

"Well, I'm hankering for a steak and a baked potato, stuffed to the hilt, and a huge salad. Does that sound good to you?"

"What is hilt?" She asked.

"It means overflowing with good things like sour cream and chives and bacon and parsley and sometimes onion bits and cheese."

She threw back her head and giggled, "All that inside one potato?"

"Yep, to the hilt." He stared into her eyes. "I love you, Inayah. Do you know that?"

"James, you don't even know me." She whispered.

"I know that you are sweet and innocent and a delicate flower that I want to protect forever." He kissed her lips, long and hard. She could feel the room spinning again, but she didn't think that it was the wine.

"James I am..."

He put his finger to her lips again, "Shh. Let me just sit here drowning in your beauty."

She shook her head, "I wouldn't want you to drown. I am not beautiful."

"Nope, you are an ugly old hag, but I love you anyhow." He laughed. "You ARE lovely." He told her again. He was mesmerized by her eyes. "You have the most beautiful eyes I have ever seen."

Little did he know that for her entire life she had learned to communicate with her eyes. Other women had their smiles and their frowns, the wrinkle of their brow, to help convey their emotions, but all she ever had were her eyes. He got lost in their depth and their beauty.

During dinner he periodically rested his hand on her thigh, but she did not remove it. Then, after dinner he helped her stand and they went out to the car. He had been walking with her hand tightly clutched in his, but then he reached across and pulled her tightly against his chest. "I want you, I need you." He whispered. "Will you marry me, Inayah?"

She felt her knees wobbling and feared that they would buckle under her. She couldn't speak. He pressed his lips to hers and nibbled on her lower lip. "I love you." He nibbled on her neck and then her ear.

She let all her feelings wash over her, like a warm rain, she said his name over and over, "James, James, James." He led her to one of the cottages and fumbled with the door. She thought, *he planned this. He knew he was going to bring me to this room.* She knew that she should protest, but with his arm around her waist, she wanted only for him to press his body against hers. She started to speak, but kept her mouth closed. She felt his fingers sliding the zipper on the back of her dress. She heard the snapping of her bra clips as he opened them. She thought she would feel embarrassment, standing there with her dress at her ankles in her partially undone bra and panties, but she did not. She watched him quickly slide off his clothes. He stood like an Adonis in front of her, nothing covering his body, but she did not look away. She let him lead her to the bed and they slid beneath the covers. He took off her bra and threw it away from the bed and then he placed his fingers gently into the elastic of the panties that barely covered her privates. She closed her eyes. She swallowed the lump in her throat. She could not change her mind now. He kissed her lips with urgency. "I love you, Inayah. I want you to be my wife."

She heard her voice, like a ghost slipping from her lips, "I love you, too, James. I want to be your wife."

They drove back in silence. He kissed her good bye. It was a long lingering kiss and then he murmured in her ear, "I don't want to leave you here," but she ran into her aunt's house before he could restrain her. Her aunt was sleeping, so she hurried into the bathroom to put on her niqab and then she went into the bedroom which her aunt had prepared for her. She rolled her dress, bra and panties into a ball and shoved them into a bag. She hung her niqab on a hook behind the door and put on a long flannel night gown that belonged to her aunt. She slid into the cold sheets and began to shiver. *What have I done? How can we ever be married? Father will never allow it.* She rolled herself into a ball and continued to shiver.

In the morning she was still wide awake as the sun peeked in through the bedroom window. She jumped up and put her feet on the cold floor. She dressed quickly into her niqab and went into the kitchen. Her aunt was sitting at the table with a cup of hot coffee steaming in front of her. She held it with both hands and blew on its surface and then tried to take a sip. "You are up, my niece. Did you sleep well?" There was a hint of a smile on her aunt's lips.

"I did." She lied.

"Have some coffee and there is bread for toast. Do you want an egg?"

Inayah shook her head. "No, just coffee." She poured herself some coffee and sat at the table with her aunt. "He wants to marry me." She announced, as she sat down.

"This is wonderful! You will marry James and not the sour old landlord." Mahibah tried to sip her coffee again.

"But my father, he paid and...." She protested, but her aunt shook her head.

"You will marry James. That is that. Money or no money. It doesn't matter my dear niece. This is your life. I won't see it destroyed like mine was." She reached out and patted Inayah's hand. "Don't worry. We will figure it all out."

She unlocked the apartment and went in. Everything seemed even more bleak than when she had left it the day before. She glanced at the chair and the couch and saw the dishes her father had left on the coffee table. She went into her room and closed the door behind her. She slowly sat on the floor, next to the window and watched through the curtain at the people going by. She didn't move for the entire day. She saw the mailman delivering letters. She saw the children coming home from school. Finally, she saw James. As always he was on his cellphone. She put her ear to the crack.

"Joe, she's wonderful. I asked her to marry me. Yes, I did. I really did and I can't wait for our wedding. Yes, I guess after I finish my studies. I would take her out more, but there is some kind of mystery about her. She meets me and we have to go somewhere far from here. Yah, it's crazy. I don't get it. I mean I have a perfectly decent apartment for her to come to." He laughed. "I don't know when. Will you be my best man? Great! No, we didn't talk about it. I feel like I am walking on air. Yes, yes, okay, laugh all you want, but I love this girl. Inayah. Yeah, she's Arabic or Egyptian or something. I don't know. Yeah, I guess she's kind of exotic. Oh stop! Okay, yeah, I'd like you to meet her." He unlocked his front door and was gone. She saw the lights in the apartment going on one by one.

"Oh James." She whispered into the room, as it became darker. She heard the front door. She knew her father would expect dinner, but she just sat there. She felt so empty. She put her hand on the cold glass. "I feel like a caged bird." She said aloud.

Her father called out, "Inayah! Where is my supper?"

"Coming father." She jumped up and went to her bedroom door, shocked when she opened it and he was standing right there. "Oh, you are home." She ventured.

"Why no dinner?" He asked.

"I slept and then I thought I will just fix it for you when you arrive. I didn't know if you would be home or not." She pushed past him as she went toward the kitchen.

"You go to your aunts and now you think you can do what you want?" She could smell the alcohol on his breath. She knew immediately that she should be extra careful in how she spoke to him. "I am the man of this house and you need to be sure my dinner is waiting."

"Yes father. I am sorry." She told him as she took ingredients for dinner out of the refrigerator. She bent over to get a pot from a lower shelf and she felt his foot against her backside and he pushed. She hit her head on the cabinet and fell to the kitchen floor.

"You are useless." He roared. "You sit in your room like a young maiden, but you do not think of your father and his needs. Well soon you will be the wife of a man not so nice as your father." He kicked her again with the toe of his boot. "I will have my dinner in front of the TV. Hurry." He added.

She scurried around the kitchen, grabbing bowls and pots and mixing this and that, her mind just a blank. She couldn't think now. If she thought, she would move slower and he would become angry. She would think later. Now she would prepare his dinner. She saw him go down the hall toward the bathroom. She continued to fry the meat, shoving it around the pan with a fork, trying to make it brown even more quickly. When he returned from the bathroom she wanted to be able to hand him his bowl of food, just to keep him happy, just to keep him from hurting her again. She waited. He didn't come back. She took the food off the burners and poured it into a serving bowl. She didn't see him come up behind her. He reached out and grabbed her niqab and pulled on it to turn her around. It pulled off her head, exposing her hair which was tightly wound into a bun.

"Think you can fool me? You think you can do what you want. What are these? What are these?" He held up her special panties with the black lace patch that just covered her privates and he held up the matching lacy bra. "These are the garments of a whore, that's what these are!" He reached for the wooden spoon on the stove, the one that had particles of food attached to it and he brought it down across her back. "You think you can disobey your father? You think you can become an American whore and no one will buy you from me?" He lit the fire on the stove and threw the panties and bra onto the flames. The panties and bra caught fire and the flames reached up into the vent. The fire alarm went off in the kitchen, blaring its loud buzzing sound. He hit her again and again, the spoon cut into her soft skin. At first she winced and cried out, but after a while she collapsed and tried to roll into a ball as he continued to hit her and kick her with his boot.

"Trash! You are no more than trash!" He kicked at her legs. She did not cry out any more, but let her mind carry her away to another place. She kept her eyes tightly closed and prayed that he would not hit her face. He didn't. He knew the landlord wouldn't want her if her face was permanently damaged. "You will wear your niqab and you will not ever come out of it and you will stay in your room and you will not see your aunt. Do you hear me? You will do as I say until your wedding day. I should kill you for this, but I need the money from the landlord. I need to get away from this place and being the lap dog for the Americans." He inhaled deeply. "That money will get me away from here. So you will do as I say and stay in your room. Do not come out, not to cook, not to go anywhere. You may go to the bathroom, this and nothing more. Do you understand me?" She had let her head drop into a nod. "Good," he said as he saw her nod. "So now we understand each other."

Mercifully, the beating stopped. She heard his heavy boots on the floor as he walked away. She heard the front door slam. She tried to stand, but couldn't. She rested her head against the cupboard. The room smelled of her burning bra and panties on the stove. He had turned off the flame, but the charred remains lay across the burner. She tried again, but still she couldn't stand. She just sat there, her entire body throbbing with pain. Hours later, she finally was able to stand by pulling herself up with her hands held tightly on the edge of the counter. She hobbled to the bathroom, locked the door and undressed. Her body was a mass of bloody cuts and dark purple bruises. She got into the shower and let the warm water caress her shoulders and run down her aching back. She cried out when the water hit the cuts along her arms and legs. She was alive, but only because he wanted the money from the landlord, otherwise, she knew that he would have killed her.

Later, she slid down to the floor and sat at the windowsill. She watched out the window into the dark street. The streetlight made eerie shadows on the street, but other than that, the streets were empty. She thought about opening the window further and then sliding out onto the sidewalk, but she sat very still. She didn't even think about James and how they had made love that day. The aching pains of her body obliterated everything, as if making love had never happened, as if she had never felt his kisses on her lips, as if she had never felt his arms tightly around her naked body. The only thing she thought about now was the throbbing pain engulfing her from her neck to her feet. She thought about her pain and she thought about how much she hated her father. This and nothing more.

Chapter 5

She watched as James came and went from his apartment. The first week after her beating, she saw him pushing his cellphone buttons, frantically trying to contact her, but her cellphone was gone. Her father had found it when he found her panties and bra. Perhaps her father was even receiving her calls and her messages from James. She had no way of knowing. She watched as James paced in front of his apartment. She heard his unsteady voice as he spoke on his cellphone, "I don't know Joe. It's been a week. I haven't seen or heard from her. I keep calling, but she doesn't answer. I left messages, but now her messages are full. I can't even leave her another message. I know, I know, but why would she disappear? I'm worried about her. What should I do, Joe?" His voice was desperate. "Yes, I know. I just can't wait. I need to speak with her aunt, but I don't know where she lives. I keep waiting for her to come into the store, but she hasn't come for over a week."

When she heard him speak of her aunt, she panicked. She pressed her ear to the crack trying to hear anything else he might say. *Should I go out and check on her,* she asked herself. She wondered if she could go and come back in before her father would even know. She listened as James continued to speak, "I keep walking the streets. Surely she isn't gone. I mean, where would she go? Well, I'm just going to go on one long drunk. Okay, who cares if it's wise. I don't give a damn if it's wise. Shit." His voice was low and tortured.

He clicked his cellphone buttons and then pushed on the screen with his fingers. He put the phone into his pocket. She watched as he disappeared into his apartment. She whispered, "I'm so sorry, James." She saw the lights go on in his apartment. She watched as he swigged a drink on a bottle of alcohol. "Oh James, please don't do this." She whispered. She stood up and made up her mind. "I need to check on my aunt." She went into the bathroom and made sure that her niqab was properly covering her face. She tiptoed in the dark to the front door. She opened the door, barely a crack, and slid her body outside. The cold wind hit her face, stinging her eyes. She started walking quickly down the street towards her aunt's house. Mere moments later, she tapped on her aunt's door.

A withered old man opened the door. She recognized her Uncle immediately. She froze. Would he tell her father? "I've come to check on Aunt Mahibah." She bravely announced.

"She isn't here. She went to visit her friend." His eyes locked on hers. "Does your father know you are out?" His voice growled. She looked at his crepe skin hanging around his neck. She saw his bony fingers holding onto the door. He was a weak old man. She shoved her hands against his narrow chest. He fell to the floor. "What are you doing?" He screamed. She stepped over him and ran into her aunt's bedroom. She found her tied to her bed. She wrapped her arms around her, "Are you alright, Aunt Mahibah?"

"Untie me," she demanded. "The ol' goat caught me off guard."

"Did he hurt you?" Inayah untied her aunt's hands. She stared at the bruise around her aunt's wrists.

"No, he just caught me unawares and then he was able to tie me here. Where is the monster?"

"I knocked him down, he is in the living room." Inayah looked nervously towards the door. She hadn't thought that he might come after her. The two women hurried into the living room. He was still laying on the floor, whimpering about his broken hip.

"You have injured my hip, you bitch! Help me up." He growled at her.

Inayah stepped over his body. "I could kill you Uncle, but I won't because of my Aunt. She may need you." She looked at her aunt, "Do you need this worm?"

Her aunt silently shook her head, "I don't need him for anything."

"Good." Inayah put her foot on the old man's neck. She pressed and watched his eyes bulge on his face. She glanced at her aunt, there was a silent smile, a tortured macabre smile on her aunt's lips. The old man began to choke and gurgle. She lifted her knee and stomped her foot down. They heard the *crunch* of his neck bones. His mouth gulped for air. His body convulsed, like a chicken without its head. Her Uncle was dead.

Her aunt put her arm around her nieces' shoulder. "Go home my dear. I will take care of his body." Her aunt pushed her out the door. "Go, hurry. Don't let your father know you have gone out." The woman glanced at her husband's body on the floor. His eyes were wide open, but it was too late for him to see.

Inayah glanced at her Uncle's body and then turned and ran down the street. She unlocked her door and slammed it shut behind her. She leaned against it, breathing heavily. The apartment was still dark. Her father would have no idea that she had gone out. She went into her room and collapsed on the floor. She rested her chin on the window sill as she looked out into the night. She put her hands on the glass and felt the cold glass cool her palms. When had she become such a brutal murderess? She looked at her hands, they seemed familiar to her, but who was this woman who murdered so easily, so effortlessly? She thought about her father. *Will I murder him too, my own father?* She saw James coming out of his apartment. He seemed unsteady on his feet. He began to shout, his tongue thick with alcohol, "Inayah! Inayah!" He began to call her name. It was evident that he was drunk. "Inayah! Where are you my love?" He came close to her window. She could open it and reach out and hug him, but she didn't. "Inayah!" he screamed. She felt her eyes fill with tears. She wiped them with her niqab. "Inayah! I love you, Inayah!" She did not move. She wanted to reach out, but she fought the urge. Her father would kill him and then he would kill her. Finally, he went back into his apartment. She saw the lights go off one by one. She put her arm on the sill and rested her forehead against it. "What am I going to do?" She closed her eyes.

She didn't hear her father come home. He didn't come into her room. He fell in a heap on the living room couch. He would tell his daughter in the morning that her Uncle had been murdered by an intruder. *Someone is murdering Arabs in the neighborhood. This is the second murder.* He wondered who would be next. Now, he needed to sleep off the alcohol in his body. Tomorrow he would have to speak to the police. His eyes drooped and he fell into a fitful sleep.

Later, in the early hours of the night, when she woke up on the window sill, she could hear him snoring in the living room. She climbed into her bed, not even bothering to remove her niqab. Tomorrow she would ask him if she could go to her aunt. She knew that he would be telling her what happened to her Uncle. She sighed as she pulled the blankets up to her chin. She tried to feel *something. Anything.* But try as she might, her mind and body was devoid of any emotion.

James didn't come out of his apartment for days. She watched and waited. She sat for hours with her eyes scanning the street, waiting for him to appear. Two weeks passed. James seemed to be swallowed up by his apartment. He didn't go out. His lights went on at night, but he rarely stood in front of the windows. She watched him guzzle a bottle of wine while he stood in his kitchen. *How can I go to him? How can I explain my bruises and my cuts?* she thought, *but I need to go to him. I need to tell him that I do love him, that I do want to be his wife. How can I do this without him wanting to kill my father or telling the police?* She was surprised by her feelings of loyalty to her father. *What do I care if James tells the police?* But she knew the answer. *If the police interview her, won't they begin to put all the pieces together?*

Then she felt an emotion. It was deep within her: *Self-preservation.*

She began to make her bed. She had tidied her room so many times in the past weeks that it was like a sterile hospital room. She felt her stomach churn and put her hand to her mouth. She ran to the bathroom and vomited into the toilet. *That's all I need, the flu.* She thought. She took a washcloth and patted her face with cool water, but no sooner had she wiped her mouth, then she vomited again. Her face turned crimson with the effort of her vomiting. She had the dry heaves and her veins bulged across her forehead. She went back to her room and laid on top of the bedspread. She lay there very still, but still her stomach churned. She ran to the bathroom again, barely making it to the toilet, but again she had painful dry heaves, since her stomach was empty. Then, finally she returned to her room. She went to the desk in the corner of her room. She opened the calendar and then, like a brick hitting her head, she saw the red circle on a date that had passed four days before. Her monthly period was late. The air was sucked from her lungs.

She whispered, "I'm going to have James' baby." She put her hands on her stomach and she felt a warm feeling flood over her. She held her hands on her stomach and closed her eyes. She waited to see if the feelings continued, but only one feeling kept coming to the surface, no matter how much she wanted to feel "love", the only feeling she had was "fear". Without another thought she went to the closet and began to pull clothes off the hangers. She yanked out a wooden hanger, a plastic hanger, and then finally, a wire hanger from the neighborhood cleaners; it was still wrapped in the triangle paper with the cleaners' name printed on the triangle: Simple Dry Clean.

She ripped off the paper and then looked at the twisted metal near the curve of the hook. She began to pull the wire apart, unraveling the wire that wrapped around the neck of the hanger. She sat down on her bed and concentrated on separating the twisted wire spirals. She thought of nothing else, but the 'job' of releasing the hanger of its grip on itself. Finally, the wire came apart and she stretched the wire out long, the length of her arm. She put the wire hanger on the bed and stood up. She stared at it, a long shiny black wire with one end slightly bent and twisted, laying on the bed. She removed her shoes and then her niqab. She went to the linen closet and removed one crisp white sheet. She didn't even think that she was standing in the hallway, exposed, if her father should come home. She went back into her room. She took the dismantled hanger in her hand and placed it on her desk. She smoothed the sheet on top of the bed, smoothing her hands over the material over and over again, making sure all the wrinkles were removed. She took her desk chair and put it against her bedroom door, shoving it under the doorknob. The door had a lock, but she was sure her father had a key. Once she felt secure that the door was now impossible to open, she removed her underwear and laid down on the white smooth sheet, holding the black hard cold wire in her shaking hand. She opened her knees, like a butterfly taking flight, and began to thread the pitiless wire into herself...

Chapter 6

A small raven hopped along the window sill, pecking at the bugs caught in a spider web in the corner. Had the bird known, when he peered into the bedroom, he would have screeched, but he ignored the body on the bed which lay motionless in a crimson puddle. The raven preened his feathers with his sharp beak, cocked his head, and then, the jet black bird flew away.

Mahibah banged on the front door. She wanted to tell Inayah that her new in-laws had arrived and were anxious to meet her. They were two withered prunes. Their gray eyes peeked over long pointed noses and their words came out of cracked ancient lips. They were well into their late eighties, but were delighted that they were finally going to have grandchildren. Neither of them really cared who their son had finally picked as a wife, only that before they died they would hold his child in their arms. The wedding was two days away and their excitement was mounting. They didn't care if his bride was ugly or beautiful, they thought only of their son's seed finally having a vessel in which his could grow into their grandchild.

Mahibah had a different plan. Her fist thudded urgently against her niece's apartment door.

"Inayah!" The aunt closed her fist as she banged even harder on the door. She had neglected her niece for the past few weeks as she made preparations for her husband's funeral. First, there had been the long interviews with police detectives. They wanted to find the murderer who had been plaguing the neighborhood, targeting Arabic individuals. The police thought the person must belong to some renegade ant-Arab gang. Though, they hadn't ruled out the infamous ISIS targeting Arabic-American citizens. Just thinking the word *ISIS* made Mahibah shiver. She banged on the door again. *Perhaps she's gone out,* she thought. She glanced across the street at James' apartment. In a careless moment, she started across the alley. She didn't care if anyone saw her. This was too important to ignore. Her niece was gone. For all she knew her brother had murdered his daughter and thrown her body in the Potomac River!

She tapped softly on James' door. When he didn't answer, she pushed the doorbell. The door opened. A straw-haired woman with bright red lipstick stood in front of the opening. She was wearing blue silk baby doll pajamas. She had a beer can in her hand. "Yeah?" She stared down at Mahibah. "What do you want? We're not buying." She said with a snarl in her voice.

"Who is it, Janelle?" Mahibah recognized James' voice in the background.

"It's a lady in one of those Arab garbs." Janelle leaned against the door as James hurriedly pushed her aside.

"Mahibah, where is she?"

Mahibah looked at his hair matted to his head; she saw the pupils of his eyes were wide and his chin was covered with jagged stubble. He hadn't shaved in days. His chest was bare and she looked down when she saw the black soft curls covering his chest.

"I don't know where she is, I was hoping you would know." She managed to speak.

The woman leaned in and kissed James' cheek, "Get rid of the old lady, sweetie. We got things to do." She grabbed onto James' arm and tried to pry him away from the door.

He shrugged off her hand, "Get away. Get dressed and leave." He turned to Mahibah. "Come in."

"I cannot. I will wait out here for you."

He nodded and closed the door softly. In moments he came outside. He had his hands in his pockets. "Do you have any idea where she might have gone?" He asked nervously.

Mahibah shook her head. "She could be anywhere. I knocked on her door, but she didn't answer. She could be at the bottom of the river."

"Tell me where she lives. I will go and see if I can find her. I could break down the front door."

Mahibah looked at him for a long time. "She lives," She paused as she looked up into his eyes. She stopped and bit her lip. Telling him where her niece lived was breaking every rule that she and her niece had put in place.

"Mahibah! This is not a time to keep it from me!" He hollered at her.

She turned and pointed across the street. "There."

"What? There? There across the alley?"

Inayah's aunt nodded her head. "That's her window." Her arm was out-stretched with her index finger pointing to Inayah's curtained window.

He gasped, "No! All this time she's been right there? She could see me when I came and when I went." He ran past Mahibah and went to Inayah's window. He tried to see through the curtains, but the room was as bright as the outside, so he couldn't see through the curtain. He put his hands into the one- inch crack and pulled up. The window slid up. He pulled the curtain aside and saw Inayah on the bed. He saw the blood beginning to brown and cake around her body. "Oh my God!" He climbed through the window. He pulled his cellphone out of his pocket and dialed 911, even before he touched her cold and clammy skin. "Inayah." He put his hand to her cheek, "Oh my sweet, Inayah." He heard the sirens coming from far away. He wrapped her in a blanket and carried her to the front door. He opened it and carried her out into the street.

Mahibah reached out to touch her niece's hair which fell like a black waterfall in front of James. "What happened?" she asked when she saw her niece's blood soaking the blanket wrapped around her.

He answered bluntly. "She killed our baby."

Mahibah stepped back and covered her mouth with the back of her hand. She spoke urgently, "Take her far from here, James. Don't let the ambulance take her. Her father will go to the hospital and kill her."

"She will die if she doesn't get medical help." He saw the ambulance coming around the corner. "I will guard her. I won't let her father near her."

The aunt looked at the ground and nodded, but she knew Inayah's father would find a way to kill her, just like he had killed their sister, but she watched as Inayah's lifeless body was put into the ambulance, as the red light created intermittent patterns of flashing red on the apartments' walls and windows. James insisted that he be allowed into the ambulance with her. When they asked if he was related to her, he told them he was her husband. He sat next to her on the small stool, holding her hand tightly in his.

He waited in the hall while doctors came in and out, followed by several nurses. Finally, a nurse gave him a white hospital shirt to cover his clothes and a mask for his face. Then, he was allowed in to see her. She was sleeping peacefully, breathing softly, her face as white as the pillow under her head. He looked up at the nurse, "Is she dying?" he asked.

The nurse shook her head, "We don't think so. She lost a lot of blood, but she seems like she will be okay. She has an infection and as long as we pump antibiotics in her and keep her fever down, we think she will recover."

He nodded and took Inayah's hand and rubbed his thumb over it softly. "Inayah, it's me darling. I'm so sorry, my love." She didn't stir. His eyes filled with tears, "I love you, my darling."

The nurse whispered, "It's hard to lose a baby." She obviously hadn't read the chart.

James didn't answer. He bent and kissed Inayah's forehead and felt the heat rise into his lips. She was burning hot. Fear began to grab his mind and his heart; *Am I going to lose her? Oh, God, please don't take her from me now.*

He heard a tap at the door and his entire body stiffened. He glanced around the small room to see what he could use for a weapon to defend her if he needed to, but there was nothing. The nurse said, "Come in." He moved forward so that he could tackle her father if he dared come near her.

"Is she alright?" He heard the voice of Mahibah.

The air gushed from his lungs in one long push. "She has a fever." He managed to say. "The nurse says she should be okay."

Mahibah stood on the other side of the bed. "Did she wake up?"

James shook his head. "She's sleeping. She lost a lot of blood."

Mahibah nodded, "She lost your baby. I'm sorry."

Her eyes met James' eyes. They both knew that Inayah had aborted the baby. Neither of them could say the truth. The tears stung James' eyes. He wanted to cry for Inayah, but in this quiet moment, a tear zigzagged down his unshaven face when he thought of the child he would never know. He felt a pressure in his chest as if an invisible hand was squeezing his heart. Inayah had murdered his child. He desperately tried to push the thought from his mind, but still persisted.

Mahibah reached across the bed and grabbed his hand. She squeezed tightly. "There will be other babies." She whispered.

How could he tell her that he mourned the loss of this baby, his first baby? How could she know what it is to love someone so completely that the thought of her having his baby consumed his every waking moment? Now, their first child was gone. That tiny precious innocent life with its teeny beating heart was taken. He collapsed into the chair behind him; he covered his eyes with his hands as he began to weep.

Mahibah rushed to his side and put her arm around his shoulders. "She will be okay," she patted his back.

But his tears were not for Inayah. His tears and sobs were for his unborn child. The child he would never know. There was no name for the pain in his heart.

By nightfall, Inayah's eyes started to flicker open. She turned to the right and saw her aunt sitting next to the bed, covered in her niqab and her Abaya. To her left, she saw James sitting next to her.

"James?" She whispered hoarsely.

"Yes, darling, I am here." He jumped up and put his hand on her head and ran his hand over her hair.

"Take me out of here, James. My father will come and kill us. Please take me out of here." She began to thrash in the bed, trying to get her legs over the side.

The nurse became alarmed, "Mam, please be still, you are connected to IV needles. Please you mustn't move like this."

"Take all the needles out. I am leaving. I have to go. James, take me out of here!"

He turned to the nurse, "Can she leave if she wants to?"

The nurse shook her head, "I'm sure the doctors don't want her to leave."

Inayah sat up and moaned, "I must get out of here. You don't understand. My father will kill us."

"Let me check with the doctor to see if we can give her a sedative." The nurse started for the door, but James grabbed her arm.

"No, ask the doctor if she can leave. I want to take her out of here."

"I'll ask." The nurse left the room.

James helped Inayah sit up. "I don't think you can walk, darling."

"Get me a wheelchair." She ordered. She turned to her aunt, "Please, watch the door. Go into the hallway and let me know if he is coming."

Her eyes scanned the room for a weapon, much the same way that James had looked, but he found none, but she did find a spoon sitting on the tray. It would have to do, if need be. She snatched it off the bedside table.

James left the room to hunt for a wheelchair. Mahibah stayed outside by the door. Inayah saw a white terry robe hanging on the outside of the bathroom door. She would have to wear that when it came time to leave since she didn't have any of her own clothes. She didn't think about what she had done. She didn't think about anything, other than that she had to leave before her father found her.

When James came back, he didn't have a wheelchair. "I can't find any. I think they have to be checked out or something. I need to go home to get my car so we can get away from here."

Her eyes became wild, "You can't leave me here."

"I have to, sweetheart. I have no choice. We don't have the car here. I came with you in the ambulance." He wanted to add, *why didn't you tell me you lived across the alley from me?* But he didn't ask her. He just stared at her pale face. It seemed as if her eyes had sunk in it and were encircled with blue. He had almost lost her forever. "I'm going to go get my car. Don't leave. You won't leave, will you, Inayah?"

She smiled at him. He knew her too well. She had thought that she might do just that, but when she placed her legs over the edge of the bed her head began to spin. She knew enough that she needed help. James and Mahibah would have to make sure she got out of there safely because she was too weak to insure it for herself.

He leaned over and kissed her lips softly. "I'm so sorry, Inayah."

She looked down at her hands gripping the blankets. "Hurry back," she said.

He turned and went out the door. Mahibah grabbed his arm, "Where are you going?"

"I'm going to get my car and take her to a special place I know where she will be safe." He pulled free from her grip. "I don't plan to take any chances. You make sure you keep your eyes open. Do you think he will find her here?"

Aunt Mahibah nodded, "Like the lion finds the lamb."

She watched James walk down the hall and enter the elevator. She took a deep breath. She wondered how she could stop her brother if he came to kill them. She began to look around for something to defend herself with, but found nothing. She peeked into the room, but Inayah was hidden behind the sliding curtain suspended on a rail around her bed. She heard the whirring and beeping of the machines that her niece was connected to. She hoped the nurse would hurry back. She didn't like that her niece was alone in the room, but she had to stay at her post, watching for her brother. She knew he would come.

The nurse came briskly down the hall, "Okay, she can't leave. The doctor says she needs the antibiotic in her IV and she has to stay." The nurse went into the room and gave the same news to Inayah. Inayah immediately began to object.

"It is a free country! That's what everyone says. You can't keep me here. I demand to see the doctor. I am going to leave." She put her legs over the edge of the bed and felt her head become light. She laid back down. "The doctor needs to give me antibiotic pills to take with me. Find him and bring him here so I can talk to him."

"But he has explicitly told me that you may not go. You are too ill to leave. You are being given very powerful antibiotics through your IV." The nurse looked at the IV bottle which was almost empty.

Inayah gritted her teeth. "Bring me the doctor."

"He will be making his rounds at seven." The nurse unhooked the bottle and started to put another one on the hook. "Just relax and let the medication work. You are going to feel great by morning."

Inayah looked into the nurse's eyes which were a bright blue peering over the face mask. "By morning, I'll be dead."

"Nonsense. You are getting better every moment." She patted Inayah's hand. "By tomorrow you can go home and you will be fine."

Inayah shook her head, "I will leave tonight. Before the doctor. Or by tomorrow I will be dead."

The nurse didn't know what to say next. This patient was obviously having delusions. "May I get you some juice or a sandwich?" She smiled, "The kitchen is closed, but I have my ways."

"No, I'm not hungry. Please nurse, can you get me a wheelchair? James will be here soon to take me and I don't think I will be able to walk down the halls."

They heard a tap at the door. The nurse said, "Yes?"

She saw the shadow in the doorway and knew immediately who it was. He came in and stood at the foot of the bed. "The neighbors told me." His eyes were black piercing marbles in his face, boring into her. "Why do I have to have the neighbors tell me that my daughter is sick?"

She didn't move, but felt for the spoon that she had put under the blankets. "I'm not that sick," She whispered.

"Blood is everywhere in the house." He answered bluntly. "What happened to you?"

"I had a female hemorrhage." Her voice was unemotional. "It happens." She added.

"Your wedding is in two days. Will you be strong by then?" he asked.

She nodded.

"Good." He then backed out of the room. He was satisfied by her answer. He saw Mahibah in the hallway. She had moved to the other side of the hall. "You!" he pointed towards his sister. "You should have told me."

"Brother, there was no time. It was an emergency."

"Yes, she told me, female hemorrhage."

Mahibah nodded. "Yes, yes a terrible female hemorrhage."

He shrugged his shoulders, "It happens." He turned and went down the hall. He pushed the elevator button and waited for the elevator. She held her breath until he disappeared into the elevator. She went into the room. "He has left."

Inayah tensed when the door opened again. "It is me, Inayah."

She knew that it was Mahibah's face, but her heart quickened. "Are you sure he has gone?"

Mahibah nodded.

"Where is James? He left a long time ago."

Her aunt went to the window. She could see all the way down the street in both directions, but she didn't see James' car arriving. The sun was going down. She could see its flame in the windows of the building across the street.

"Do you see the car?" Inayah asked.

Her aunt shook her head. She pressed her forehead against the cold glass. She silently hoped James would hurry. She knew her brother would begin to think and then he would return. He would kill Inayah and he would kill her. She knew her brother. Sometimes he took longer to think things through, but he was a smart man. He would be able to figure it out.

The room's door banged open. Inayah and Mahibah saw the wheelchair first. Then they saw James pushing it with a big smile on his shaved face. "I took a little longer to make myself presentable to my sweetie." He pulled the chair next to the bed. "Your chariot, my lady." Mahibah hurried to the bathroom door and got the white terry bathrobe.

"Here put this on her. Oh, we have to remove those needles!" She lifted Inayah's arm. "The nurse should do this. We don't want any more blood pouring out of you."

"She went to get me a tray of food." Inayah looked at the needles in her arms. "I think I can take these out." She pulled on the needle and her mouth let out a small gush of air as she felt the needle leave her skin. She held her hand tightly over it. "Get me a bandage from that drawer under the table." Her aunt handed her the bandage. She quickly put it over the hole in her arm and continued to press on it. "I'll be ready in a moment." She slid her feet over the side. James put on her shoes and then helped her into the white terry bathrobe.

"I should have brought you some clothes to wear, but we will take care of it later." He then helped her into the wheelchair. "Mahibah, what are you going to do?"

The older woman shrugged her shoulders. "I guess I will take a taxi to the airport. I hear that Florida is a nice place." She kissed her niece's cheek. "I will miss you, my dear niece."

"How will I find you?" Inayah's voice cracked with her emotion.

Her aunt shook her head, "It is safer if we don't see each other, my dear. Safer for both of us. Your father has many eyes. If we were together it would be easier to find us." She hugged her. "We will see each other in the afterlife when we see your mother again." She continued to hold onto Inayah's neck. "I love you, my little bird." She kissed her cheeks again and again. Finally, James had to wheel the chair away from her and out the door.

"Be careful, Mahibah." He said as he went into the hallway. He rolled the chair swiftly to the elevator. He didn't turn and look at Mahibah. He knew she would be standing in the doorway watching them leave. He lifted his eyes to the elevator monitor above the doors and watched the numbers rise. Ten, eleven, and finally the twelfth floor. The doors squawked open.

Inayah's father was standing in the middle of the elevator, his eyes glaring straight into them. Without any thought Inayah stood and lunged forward with her spoon held backwards in her hand, exposing the square handle. She plunged the handle of the spoon deep into his stomach. As he doubled over, James pushed the chair quickly into the elevator and jammed his fingers on the down button. They watched as her father fell to the floor clutching his stomach. Then the doors closed like a curtain on the last scene of a play. She hoped her aunt wouldn't wait, but take the next elevator down, but she couldn't think about that now. James was pushing the wheelchair so quickly that it seemed all the people just sped past them. In no time he was helping her into the front seat of his car. He gave the wheelchair a push and sent it careening into a car that was next to theirs. He backed the car out of the parking space quickly and within moments they were headed down the street and in a few more minutes were speeding down the freeway. He glanced at Inayah as she pushed the buttons on her seat so that she could recline. He reached over and took her hand, "You okay, baby?" He asked.

She nodded. "I just need to sleep for a few minutes."

"Yes, sleep darling. It's a long ride." She didn't hear him answer, she was already sleeping. She didn't wake up until she heard the ignition of the car turn off.

"We're here." He smiled. "Not bad for a four-hour drive."

"I slept four hours?"

"Yep. How do you feel?" he asked.

She placed her hand on her stomach, "I feel empty."

He nodded as he looked into her sad eyes. She whispered, "I will always feel empty."

Chapter 7

When he put the key into the lock, the door creaked open. He pushed the door with his foot. A musty heavy scent met their noses. Inayah coughed and put her hand over her mouth and nose. "It hasn't been opened in years." He offered as an apology. "My grandfather died six years ago and left it to me. I haven't been here since." The oak planks groaned under their feet. He left her in the entry as he opened the sooty drapes and slid open the windows. He spoke quickly, "I know it doesn't look like much, but it's really nice. The four bedrooms are upstairs and it has the most delightful kitchen." He looked at her, wondering if she liked the house. "So?"

She nodded. "It's lovely." She pulled the collar of the white bathrobe tightly around her neck. "Really. It just needs a major cleaning."

"And that's my plan. I am going to clean it top to bottom. Right now I need to go cut us some wood for the fireplaces. There's one in the master and one in the living room. We don't have any other heat in the house. Will you be okay while I go to the woods and cut some firewood?"

She walked to the couch which was covered by a large dusty white sheet. She pulled on it and revealed a burgundy chenille couch. "I'll just sit here and wait for you."

He laughed, "I know it's a bit overwhelming, but once things are cleaned up, I think you are going to love living in the woods. There's no one for miles. We will be safe here." He smiled. He bent over her head and kissed her. "Okay, sit there and I'll be back in a few minutes."

"James, are there some clothes?" She asked just as he was about to close the front door.

"Maybe some of my grandma's old clothes are still in the upstairs closet. We can take a look when I get back." He winked at her and closed the door.

Together they worked on cleaning the house. Days piled onto days. James repaired the broken kitchen stool so she could sit and stir food on the stove. She wore his grandmother's gingham dresses with the white kitchen apron. She pinned up her long hair using a tortoise comb she found in a drawer upstairs. In the evening, there was no electricity so she lit candles. He stuffed logs into the fire box of the stove. "We even have an old washtub for scrubbing our clothes." He looked at her for approval, but she was frowning.

"You mean we don't have to go down to the river and beat them against rocks?" She asked sarcastically.

"Of course not, silly!" He chucked under her chin with his fingertips.

"James, that's sarcasm. I can't believe we don't have electricity." She shook her head.

"We have it, but we don't have the ability right now to turn it on. I think it will be too dangerous to go to town and interact with people. I am even waiting to go to town to get groceries. There are a few more staples in the pantry and I will get us some game."

She opened her mouth to speak, but then closed it abruptly. If her mouth had been a hinged door it would have snapped loudly. She thought of the large sack of flour she had found in the back of the pantry—it was crawling with weevils. There were too many to sift through them. She had thrown the flour out back. She closed her eyes and began to stir the pot of soup on the stove. She had found a few onions in the garden and used spices and a cube of beef bouillon. It would be a watery version of French onion soup. Their meals had been sparse, but each day she was able to concoct variations of palatable meals with what she found in the pantry. There were a few wild chickens who roosted in the barn, so she gathered eggs for omelets.

She watched him leave through the kitchen's back door. He was going to find some *game* and more firewood. *Am I locked in the 18th century?* She asked herself, as she began to stir the pot even more vigorously. She looked out through the large bay kitchen window at the yard. James had moved the car into a barn in the back, so all she saw were trees surrounding the house. The farmhouse was definitely isolated. She let out a sigh. She would be safe here, there was no doubt in her mind about that.

He returned with his arms full of firewood. He made two trips outside to bring more wood into the house and then he brought in two dead rabbits that he held by their ears. "The trap worked." He grinned. He put the rabbits in the sink. "I'll skin these a little later, right now, my love, what I want to do is ravish your body with my mine." He wrapped his arms around her and squeezed tightly. "I missed you." His hands cupped her breasts. "I want to take you upstairs."

"Now?" She tried to wiggle from his embrace.

"Right now." He turned her around and kissed her mouth. He sucked gently on her lower lip. "I love you Inayah." He took her hand and led her up the stairs. She held back, so he gently pulled her. Her mind began to race, *The last thing I want now is another baby.* There were no rubbers in the bathroom cabinet, she had checked. When he lifted her up and plopped her gently on the big four poster bed, the air gushed out of her lungs. "Are you sure we should do this now, James?" She asked.

"Why not darling?" His lips nibbled on her neck and then he undid the buttons of the gingham dress. His hand reached inside the opening and cupped her warm breast in his hand. She closed her eyes and let the feelings wash over her. In spite of her initial reluctance, she felt her body command her to attention as he slid his hand over her stomach.

"Oh James," she whispered.

Every time he made love to her, she got lost in the scent of his body, the urgency of his touch, and her mind seemed to swoon, washing away any other thoughts that she was having. Her hips eagerly raised to meet his. The sounds of the birds in the trees outside disappeared; the creaking of the rooftop disappeared, the wind rustling the trees disappeared...there was nothing but the sound of his heavy breathing blended into hers with murmurs of , "Oh yes, oh sweetheart yes."

Then, weeks later he announced that he was going to town. "I am going to take a load of wood to sell and get us some real groceries. What would you like?"

"You mean anything?" she asked.

"Yes, anything."

"Fruit? Oh, and some yogurt." She patted her hands together like a child. "And flour without weevils and yeast to make bread."

"Sweetheart, I believe it's extra anyhow to buy flour with weevils. They charge for the added protein. It is protein enriched flour." His face was serious.

"Really? Oh James, I'm so sorry. I threw out the protein enriched flour! I thought that they were bad worms and I didn't want to cook with it. There were so many! I have never eaten protein enriched flour before."

He began to laugh so hard that his eyes teared.

"You were teasing me, weren't you? You are terrible!" She punched his arm with her fist.

He winced, "Ow. You don't even hit like a girl, you are one strong broad."

She laughed, "When I must be, I am." She turned away from him, "Don't tease me like that again, okay?"

He kissed her lips softly. "No guarantees," he curled her long hair around his hand. "You bring out the devil in me, sweetie, what can I say?"

She let his deep hard kiss take over her body. She wanted to take HIM upstairs, but he pulled away. "I won't be gone long. I hope I can sell the wood, then we can have even more weevil-less flour." He laughed.

"Stop it! James you are so mean to me." She stuck out her lower lip in a pout.

"Baby, I'm sorry. I love you and you just are so much fun to tease." He slapped her bottom as he headed for the back door. "Lock the doors. I will be home in about an hour or so."

She grabbed his hand, "You promise?"

He returned to face her; he grabbed her hands in his and held them tightly in front of her, "I promise." He let her hands drop from his as his hand brushed her damp curls from her brow. "With yogurt and fruit in hand." He kissed her lips again. "Don't worry, darling. Everything is okay now."

She nodded. "Okay then. See you soon." She watched him leave and then quickly latched the door. She kept watching out the window as the car came out of the barn and started down the dirt road. She went into the living room and looked at all the books on the shelf. She took a book from the shelf and began to flip through its pages. She liked looking at pictures and it had lots of colorful pictures. She went into the kitchen and put a kettle on for tea. Dusk's shadows began to move through the yard. *James has been gone a long time,* she thought, as she lit a candle. Then, she saw it. A long black limousine was parked in front of the house. Her hand cupped quickly against her lips! She grabbed a knife from the kitchen drawer. She knelt down under the window, griping her fingertips on the windowsill as she watched through the curtain to see who was in the car, but the windows were stained black. *Is the person out of the car?* She asked herself. She glanced towards the kitchen door. *Should I go out this door?* A shiver went through her body. *What if the person is by the back door? Or is the person at the front door?* Her heart pounded against her chest. She heard a car door slam. Then she heard another car door slam. "There are two of them," she hissed aloud. She ran to the kitchen door and yanked it open. She ran out the door and into the woods.

She didn't hear the familiar voice, "Inayah! Open the door! Inayah, it's your father and your husband- to- be. Open the door, we know you are in there."

Inayah kept running. She jumped over twigs, she sprinted through piles of fallen leaves. She heard several gunshots echoing through the woods. She jumped into a stream, walking upstream, knowing that if she was followed they would think she would go down the mountain, rather than upstream. She began to slosh through the icy water. She tried to stay near the edge of the stream to avoid any hidden deep holes. She kept climbing up, over huge boulders. Her knees were bleeding. She kept going. She didn't glance behind her. She had one goal, to put as many miles she could between her and the farmhouse before it became totally dark.

The sun disappeared and plunged her into total darkness. She got out of the stream and sat on a rock. She saw the stars and a sliver of moon over her head. She had no idea how long she had been running. Her body began to shiver. She settled her back against the boulder, facing the water from where she had just climbed.

She would have a long night, with plenty of time for her to be tortured by her thoughts. She knew that James would be returning to the farmhouse only to find those two intruders waiting for him, or perhaps the reason he was so late in returning to her was that they had already murdered him. Her teeth chattered against each other as her body's temperature continued to fall. She knew she had to find better shelter or she would die of exposure before morning. She climbed off the rock and headed deeper into the woods. She began to dig a hole with her hands, clawing at the earth. Then, she filled the bottom of the deep hole with a cavernous layer of leaves. She put a tall band of leaves along the edge of the hole. She took off her dress and hung it on a branch. She climbed into the hole and covered her naked body with the leaves that she had piled along the edges. She felt for the cold steel of the knife along her leg. She wrapped her fingers around the handle. She stared up at the stars peeking through the branches of trees. She lifted her arms and scooped up the leaves on each side of her, covering her face with the dry leaves and then, she quickly buried her arms in the sides of the hole. She continued to shiver, until she fell asleep.

Chapter 8

The warm sun managed to bypass some of the trees and shone in blotches on the ground. The golden rays, with particles dancing, shone down on Inayah's feet and on her head under the pile of dried leaves. Her dress, still hanging on the branches of a tree, had dried in the wind. She began to climb out of the hole, shaking the golden yellow and reddish orange leaves off her naked body. She brushed with her hands along one arm and then the other. She stomped her feet to remove any leaves or dirt clinging to her legs. She slipped the dried gingham dress over her head; found her underwear and her shoes which were still slightly damp, but they also had somewhat dried during the night's wind. She secured the knife into the waistband of her underwear. She saw the distinct trail of her footprints leading up to her leaf-filled grave. She stretched her arms up toward the light streaming through the branches of the trees. "Okay." She said aloud. "Now I must find my way to the road." But she went first to the icy stream and washed her face and hands. She drank small sips of the cold water. She knew she had to climb up to a high peak to see where she was and to see if she could see any roads below. No one had followed her during the night. She sighed. James was undoubtedly dead laying in the cold pool of his own blood. Her father and her intended husband, the landlord, would undoubtedly not give up until they found her. She had to go where no one would know her, some place with thousands of people crammed on the head of a pin. She would make her way to New York.

The road wasn't far from the peak, but few cars traveled along it, as was the case with most country backroads. She stood with her thumb out and with her knee bent, like she had seen hitchhikers do in the movies. It wasn't long before an old black pick-up slid to a halt. The man had on a red baseball cap and was vigorously chewing his gum. "Hey sweetheart, what are you doing way back here in the woods all by yourself?" He was young and his blue eyes twinkled when he saw her. She stood there staring at him and finally found her voice, "I need a ride into New York."

"Well little lady, I can't get you all the way to New York, but I can take you part of the way, hop in." He reached over and pushed down the handle of the door to let her in. His eyes crawled over her body.

"I'm Zeke." He winked at her. "Feel free to crank that window closed if it is too cold."

She blinked her eyes at him, like a lost kitten that he had just rescued from a rain storm, and then she turned toward the window to crank it closed. "I am Sally." She looked into his eyes. "My car broke down about ten miles back."

He grunted, "Hmm. I didn't see any cars on the side of the road." He pulled out onto the highway.

"Maybe a tow truck already took it away." She offered and then turned her head forward to look out the windshield.

He nodded, "Yah, maybe, and maybe not. Are you running away from someone, sweetheart?" He gunned the engine as they climbed a hill.

She didn't answer.

"Do you have a mean husband or something and you are running away?" He asked again.

She nodded. "Yes. I am running away from him. He is evil and hurtful and I have to get to my mother's house in New York." She fidgeted with her fingers in her lap.

"That's what I figured. I mean, a pretty gal like you hitchhiking in a little country dress. I mean, come on. You are running, that's what I figured."

She whispered, "And you are right."

"Well, I will get you to where you can catch a bus or a train. Do you have any money?"

She shook her head.

"Oh geesh woman, no one should leave without a plan to have some money. I can buy you a bus ticket."

She smiled at him shyly. "Thank you."

"Just paying it forward. I live up here on a ranch. I'm what you call a hired hand. I do odd jobs for the farmer. I just hauled some of his produce." He smiled at her. "You sure are pretty. Beautiful hair." His eyes saw the leaves still clinging to the strands of her hair. "Did you take a tumble?" He reached over and pulled a leaf out of her hair.

She nodded. "I fell."

He shook his head. "Well, you just settle back and relax and I will get you to the bus station." She put her hand on the edge of the window and looked out at the passing trees. She was headed far away from the farmhouse into the hive of bees. She would get lost in that hive and no one would ever be able to find her.

An hour later they pulled into a bus station. "I'll go get you a ticket into New York. Wait here." He left her in the truck. When he returned he was grinning and waving a ticket in the air. "Piece of cake." He told her with a huge grin on his face. "Your bus leaves in about twenty minutes. I'll wait until you get on."

She shook her head, "No, you don't have to. You've done so much for me already."

"Heck, no problem, Sally." When he said the name, he paused and shook his head, "That's not your real name, is it?"

She didn't answer.

He had parked behind the bus station. There were few cars in the parking lot. She glanced around nervously. Of course, her father would be checking all the exits out of the area, but he couldn't be in all places at once, but he could be here. She didn't see the black limo. Satisfied that she was safe, she turned to look at Zeke. He was a handsome young man with bright intelligent eyes. Initially she had feared for her safety, but he was kind and sweet. He reached out and patted her hand. "You're going to be okay. Just as soon as you get to your mama's house all this will be behind you. Here." He handed her a twenty-dollar bill. "You might get hungry." She felt him press the twenty dollars into her hand. His fingers were warm.

"I can't," she objected.

"Yes you can. You may need it. Just remember to pay it forward to someone else along the way."

She clicked open the door handle. She reached into the waistband of her underwear. She felt the cold steel of the knife. Within seconds she brought the knife into his chest. He shook his head in disbelief as he watched the blood gush onto his lap and onto the seat. "I'm sorry." She stated, as she saw his eyes mercifully close. Unfortunately, she had had a glimpse of her father as he killed the man who had helped them find their way out of the hiding place with her mother. She blinked her eyes. *I won't think about my mother*. It seemed centuries ago. She knew now that her father was right when he killed the man. Now, she was right in killing this man. This man in the red baseball cap was the only man in the whole world who knew she was going to New York. He was the only man who knew her face; the only man who could describe her to her father or to the police. Now, he was speechless. "Good bye, Zeke." She hurried to the bus. She did not look back.

Chapter 9

She walked from the bus station to Lydid Avenue, in the Bronx. She walked along the street, hearing snippets of Albanian tongue. She was smack in the middle of what is known as Little Albania. The scent of the familiar foods filled the air. As her head spun from side to side, as she tried to absorb everything within her view, she bumped into a blond muscular woman.

"Watch where you're going, bitch!" The woman gave her a shove that almost sent her to the cement under her feet.

"I'm sorry." She said quickly.

"Yah, well I can make you feel even sorrier." The woman sneered. Inayah thought perhaps the woman was Russian. She didn't have an accent, but she was so tall and muscular that she felt that she was one of those Russian experiments with male features. She groped into the recesses of her mind. *What are those humans called? Hermaphrodites.* She wondered, *Is this woman a hermaphrodite?*

"What you staring at, bitch?" The woman gave her another shove. "What are you anyhow, dressed in that flimsy checkered dress like you was going to some Bible-banger's meeting."

Inayah started to speak, but held her tongue.

"Are you new to New York, like a little lost lamb?" The woman stepped back and Inayah saw her flex her arm muscles. "I think you are lost. Are you lost?" She laughed.

"I have run away from my husband." She blurted.

The woman's eyes suddenly became softer. "Did he beat you?" She asked.

Inayah nodded.

"Shit." The woman draped her arm around Inayah's shoulders. Inayah looked into the woman's face and saw the five-o'clock shadow of a beard. "You can come with me. I will introduce you to some good people." She tightened her arm around the small shoulders of the *little lost lamb*. "Do you read? The *Gazeta Dielli* has pointed out that little lambs get killed when they come to New York without any place to go."

"I have my mother in..." Inayah began, but thought better of her lie. "You are right. I have no place to go."

"Are you Muslim?" the woman leaned in close to Inayah's face.

Inayah nodded.

"Where's your niqab?" The woman laughed.

"If you know where one is, I would like to have one. I lost mine along the way."

The woman's eyes narrowed. "Did you now? That's very interesting. By choice or did someone rip it off you?"

Inayah swallowed, feeling a lump within her throat. "I killed my infant."

The woman released her hold of Inayah's shoulders. "You killed your child?"

"Inside, I killed it." She put her hands on her stomach.

The woman shook her head, "I'm sorry. Come with me. You can speak with my boss, George. Maybe he will give you a job."

"You would do that for me, a stranger?"

"Sure. You're from the motherland, right? We have to stick together, don't we?"

"Yes, I am, how did you know?" Inayah didn't know which 'motherland' the woman was speaking of, but she thought it best that she agree with her new-found *friend.*

"Come with me. I will take you to George and get you a niqab. There are over 30 mosques within a short distance of each other. Most are Sunni." She smiled. "We gotta get you out of those clothes." She laughed again, which made Inayah laugh.   She followed the woman through the streets and alleys. They came to a mosque. "Wait here." The woman went to the side of the building and spoke with a woman who was walking in the shadows. Then, she came back with a niqab over her arm. "Let's get you into this." They hurried to a gas station and Inayah disappeared into the bathroom.   When she came out her body was covered from head to foot, except for her eyes. "That's better." The woman smiled. "Now we'll go see George and you will be more marketable."

"What?"

"Don't worry about it. I'll explain later." They went down a dark alley and the woman knocked on a dented steel door. "It's Shirley." The door swung open and Shirley and Inayah walked in. "Is George around? I have a greenie for him."

"He's upstairs. What do you know about this broad? She could be a plant."

"You are such a worry wart. She isn't a plant. I just picked her up off the street. Look at her. Does she look like a plant?"   The woman pointed towards Inayah.

The man shook his head. "Don't know what she looks like under that outfit." He lifted the hem of the skirt with his foot. "What you got under there, Toots? Got something good, I'll bet. You got something good under there?"

Inayah's eyes narrowed. She vowed if she had to kill anyone else today it would be this man.

"Whoa, little lady looks like one tough cookie." He laughed as he gave her a shove. "Take the elevator on up and you can speak with George. He likes little feisty whores like you." He threw back his head and laughed even louder. She noticed how his Adam's apple jutted out, as if it was a target going up and down in the middle of his neck as he spoke.

George was sitting at a large mahogany desk. Everything on the desk was in neat piles. He sipped from a teacup which was decorated with small roses. "What do we have here, Shirley? Did you bring me some fresh meat?" His eyes locked on the woman in the niqab. He liked the mystery of those broads, everything hidden under a big tent like that only made him want to rip it off that much more quickly. He imagined her naked body brushing the material and he got even more excited.

"She's a lost lamb, George. I thought I would bring her to you."

He nodded, "You did good, Shirley. You may go. Leave the lamb with me."

Inayah shook her head, "No, Shirley stays." Her voice was deep and commanding. "Shirley, don't move. Let's see what Mr. George has to say."

The man laughed, "I like your spunk, kid. I also like how you called me Mr. George. You got some class under that thing, not to mention a lot else going on under there. But Shirley, you've got to leave, I insist. I got business with this gal." Shirley obeyed and promptly left the room. George laughed so hard that he hit his head on the wall behind his desk. "Do you know who I am?"

Inayah thought, The man I am going to kill next?

"I'll give you a little clue. I grew up in Montenegro. I'm Albanian." He paused to let it sink in. "I came to America, through the back door in 1965. I had nothing. I'm an immigrant success story." He laughed. "So, have you heard of me?"

Inayah shook her head.

"Does Yellow House mean anything to you?" His eyes narrowed.

She could feel her knife against her thigh. Her thoughts scrambled for her attention. First, she thought of just slicing his throat quickly, but then she tuned into his words when he said *Yellow House*. Now she understood. He was that big Armenian kingpin she had read about, the one who had been accused of human body part trafficking. *Yes, I know who you are,* she thought. *You are the body snatcher.*

The man pulled up his shirt and was pointing to his scar. "Kidney." He announced proudly. "One of the first." When he grinned she knew she was standing in front of one of the most evil men she had ever set her eyes upon. He continued, "The guy donated it willingly after I found out his blood type matched mine." He grinned and his bright teeth reminded her of a jack-o-lantern, only none of his teeth were actually missing. She wondered if his teeth were *donated*, too. "Aren't you a little curious about me?" She watched as he ran his hand through his hair. He obviously knew he was good-looking and probably had a slough of girlfriends. "So where you from, Toots?"

"My name is Sally." She announced.

"Uh huh and my name's Jack-Be-Nimble." He laughed again. "You're in a niqab, for Pete's sake. That's a tip off right there. But I'll say one thing, little lady, I like you and when I like someone I am reeeeallllly nice to them." He continued laughing. "Take off the hood. I want to see your face."

Inayah's eyes looked down. She decided to play her *demure and secretive card.*

"Oh, bashful. I like that, too." He reached out and tried to lift her veil.

"Not nice." She said as she slapped his hand.

"Spunk! I like spunk, too." His eyes twinkled as he watched her with amusement, like a cat observing a bird before he eats it. "Why don't you and I go to my room for a little fun?" He coyly asked.

She put her hand against her leg, feeling the bulge of her knife for security. "Why not?" She asked with a lilt in her voice.

"Why not, indeed." He took her by the elbow and led her down a hallway to a set of double doors. He released her elbow as he swung both doors open. The foyer had marble floors and a mahogany round small table with a huge fresh bouquet of roses in the middle of it. Her eyes glanced up at the Venetian crystal chandelier above the table and the matching wall scones. "Go on in." He ordered.

Her feet slid on the marble and he caught her before she fell. Her hands rested on his chest. Her quick breaths puffed her niqab in and out as she tried to regain her composure. "Easy little lady." He whispered. He guided her into an enormous sitting room with white couches and chairs. She looked out the floor to ceiling windows which covered one whole wall at the opposite end of the room. She could see the streets of the city below. She tried not to reveal how impressed she was.

"Would you like a drink?" George was already moving toward the bar. "Name your drink." He put two glasses on the bar.

"I don't drink." She answered.

"Really? Not even water?"

"I'll have water." She nodded, "With ice."

He reached below the bar and brought out an ice bucket and put it on the bar. He poured water from a crystal pitcher over the ice. "I have bourbon if you would like bourbon and water."

She shook her head.

He handed her the glass of water. "Please, take off your veil. Get comfortable. I know you aren't religious."

"Really?" She took her hand and in one swoop took off her veil. "And how did you figure that out?"

"You are a woman who was out on the streets of New York alone. I hardly believe that your father or your husband or your brothers would approve." He poured straight bourbon into a glass for himself.

"I have no father, no husband, or brothers."

"Not even an intended?" he asked. She thought she heard a tone of mocking in his voice. Maybe he knew who she was. She stepped back towards the front doors. He laughed again, "Have I hit a nerve?" he asked.

"I need to be going. I don't believe you and I have any business to conduct." She put her hand on the doorknob and turned it. It swung open revealing a guard at the door. The guard closed the door. "Am I a prisoner now?" she asked.

George walked slowly over to the windows and stared out thoughtfully, his bourbon glass held tightly in his hand. "Sometimes I look out and watch all those people walking down there and I imagine that they are all ants and that I am a huge ant eater." His voice was low. "I have a choice. I can swoop down and eat them all at once or I can pick them off one at a time." He took a sip of his drink. "Or I can pick one at a time for my amusement and then when I am done with it, I can consume it."

She leaned against the doors. Her heart beat quickened. It's now or never. She thought. Either I kill him now or I am doomed to be his next ant.

Her hand pressed against her leg. He turned to look at her. "You are very pretty without your niqab, but I want you to promise me that I am the only one who will be allowed to remove your veil. I want to be the only one who sees those pink soft full lips." He stared into her eyes with such an intensity that she had to glance away. "The truth is that you will willingly sleep with me. It is only a matter of time. Maybe weeks, maybe days, maybe hours," he paused, "Maybe in a matter of moments."

He watched her. When she raised her hand to push back her hair, his eyes followed her hand.

"The thing is, I am a Kyre." When he didn't see any recognition in her face he said, "I am a mafia boss. I am the boss of one of the fifteen Albanian families. I am making you an offer. I am asking you to willingly join my fis." Again, he saw no recognition. "My family clan." He put his glass on the table and then walked towards her. "I know you are not Albanian, but this is not necessary. What IS necessary is your total allegiance to me." He lowered his voice, "I ask that you have total loyalty to the family. We operate under Besa."

Inayah had heard of Besa. Her father's friends had spoken of it in their secret meetings. Now it was all clear to her. Her father had once dealt with the Albanian mafia and now with her here it was all coming full circle. She wondered if George knew who she was. He was asking her to operate within the code of honor and trust which was sacred between family members as they protected you with their life and expected the same of you. She took a step towards him, "How do you know you can trust me? How do you know I won't want to cut your throat?"

"Because your reputation proceeds you."

"And how do you know that?" Her eyes held his and did not blink.

"Because I know everything." He answered bluntly. "I am a good judge of human character." He stated. "One doesn't become a Kyre without having this ability."

She started to shake her head in disbelief, but he reached out and grabbed her arm. "I have eyes everywhere, Inayah."

When he said her name her knees almost buckled under her.

"I am asking for a mik." His voice had almost turned into a growl. "Do you know this word?" His fingers tightened around her wrist. "We will have a liaison, a bond of trust between us." His fingers squeezed even more tightly. "I know you, Inayah. I know what you are capable of. I can use you and you in turn will use me."

"Why would I want this?" she asked.

"Because of who you are."

"You want me to whore for you." She tried to yank her wrist free from his grasp.

"Let's just say I want you to entice certain people to your lair, but you do not have to give them what they seek. You must only give me what I seek from them."

"I don't live by riddles!" She managed to break free and went into the middle of the room. "Who do you think you are bringing me up here to your chambers thinking that you will not only have sex with me, but ask favors of me in return! I am not chattel to pass around at will."

His hand went to his moustache and he twirled the end, "Aren't you?"

She fell to the couch and sat on the edge. The reality was that she was chattel from the moment of her birth. Now James was dead and her father and intended were out looking for her. She had nowhere to hide. She had no family and no friends. She glanced up at the stranger in front of her. This man was offering her status within his family. He was offering her protection even though she is Iraqi. The offer wasn't one of friendship, it was an offer of becoming *family.* No matter how much she just wanted to agree to his desires, her mind kept asking the nagging question of *why? Why is he interested in me? What does he want with me?*

He reached down and took her hand and lifted her up off the couch. "Come, go into the bedroom, shower and relax. Then we will talk."

She asked, "Why? Why do you want me?"

"Let's not talk business until you are refreshed." He led her to the double doors of the bedroom. "Go in, I will not bother you. Relax. You will find clothes in the closets. Take your pick. Shall I send in a maid to draw your bath?"

She wanted to resist, but she could still feel the crusted dirt from her leaf-filled grave clinging to her body. He continued to speak, but her mind hung on the thought of washing away all her previous memories by merely taking a bath. He added, "I have work to do, but I will return in a few hours. You can sleep, if you like."

He gently shoved her into the bedroom and then silently closed the doors behind her. She tried to open them again and the doors swung open, but George was gone. She wandered around the living room, then she went to the exit doors and opened them, expecting to see the guard standing there, but he was gone. She closed the doors and went back into the living room. "There is no guard," she said aloud. "What is with this guy?" She snatched a remote control off the table and turned on a television which was almost hidden in a wall shelf. She flipped through the channels and then turned the TV off again. She went into the bedroom, closed and locked the doors behind her.

She poured bubble bath salts and oils into the huge tub. She pushed the Jacuzzi button and watched as the water swirled and churned, causing mounds of bubbles to form and rise to the edge of the tub. She slipped off her clothes and slid her aching body into the bubbles. She didn't care that the water gushed over the sides of the tub onto the marble floor. She closed her eyes and let the bubbling water caress her and soothe her. She began to put the thoughts of the past into neat compartments within her brain, locking each one tightly before moving on to the next. When she came to memories of her Aunt Mahibah, she lingered on the memory of her gentle face, her warm embrace and the kisses she had given her on her cheeks. She savored the love she felt for this dear sister of her mother. She let herself absorb the love and then, just like the other memories of murder and blood, she stored Mahibah away, locked her in the deepest part of her mind where she had also put her mother. She symbolically threw away the key to this cabinet. She submerged her head under the water and held her breath for as long as she could. She heard the echoes of the jets in her ears. Everything was gone. When she rose out of the water, she was the Phoenix arising from the ashes. She briskly ran the white fluffy towel over her naked body, rubbing hard on her skin.

Then, and only then, was she able to turn her anticipative thoughts towards, George…

Chapter 10

George was an adept lover. She enjoyed his caresses and felt confident that everything he taught her she could use again. He had his expectations of her and she promised him that she would not disappoint him. "My dear, you do not have to follow through with anything, you know this. I only want you for myself. You are mine. You will merely draw the fly into my web. Can you do this, my dear?"

She nodded silently. "I will bring those you want to you, George." Her head lay in the crook of his arm. He pulled her closer until her naked body pressed against his. "You don't have to worry; I know what you want me to do."

His hand squeezed her arm, "But you will not let him touch you. No one should touch this skin." He opened his palm and caressed her arm, rubbing his hand over the smooth skin. "You are mine and only mine." He bent his head to kiss her lips. "And no one should kiss these lips, or see what I see."

She nodded. "I know, George."

Suddenly, he jumped from the bed. "Oh! I almost forgot. I have brought you a present." She watched as he went to the pocket of his suit jacket. He came back to the bed and meticulously unfolded a tin foil packet. "This is some really good stuff that I just had smuggled into the country. I saved some for you."

She looked at the white powder now exposed on top of the tinfoil.

"Drugs?" She asked in shock.

"The best cocaine you will ever try." He smiled. "And I saved it for you."

Had he been a vulture saving the best carrion for her, she wouldn't have been pleased. "I don't do drugs." She boldly stated.

"Try it my sweet. For papa." He kissed her forehead. "Just a wee bit. Sniff it up your nose. Go on. Papa will be watching." He reached out and brushed her cheek with his hand, but she did not move. His voice became even sweeter and softer, "Please my darling, just try it. If you don't like it, you don't ever have to do it again." He lifted it up. "Or maybe just taste it with your finger?"

She shook her head. "I don't want this." Her eyes met his. "Please, George."

"Uh uh, don't say no to Papa now my love." He quickly left for the bathroom and returned with a mirror. "I am going to put it here for you and you will sniff some of it up into your nose. Haven't you done this before?" He asked. He handed her a straw. "Use this."

She shook her head again. "I don't do drugs."

His voice became deep and gurgled in his throat, "Try it now." He ordered with finality in his voice. He reached out and grabbed her hair, pulling on it, making her wince. "Now."

She took the straw in her shaking hand. She closed her eyes and sniffed a small amount into her nose. It instantly slammed against the nerve endings in her brain and washed over her. He watched her reaction with a smirk of pleasure on his face and then he began to run his hands over her body gently. "You liked it, right?" He asked.

In her fog she murmured, "I don't like drugs."

From that moment on he always offered her drugs before he made love to her. He explained and rationalized that it made her relax and become more responsive to his touch. She didn't argue any more and often began to anticipate their love making, if only to have her fix each night and morning. She found herself expectant and eagerly awaiting his arrival, but not for his attention, but for the hit of the drugs that she had come to want and eventually, need, to be able to think and function.

He didn't take her out of the apartment, but made sure she had anything she wanted. When she asked for green ice cream, he brought her spumoni. When she asked for furs, he brought her minks. When she whimpered that he never took her anywhere, he wiped her tears and told her he wanted her all to himself and that she should understand this. "I love you my sweet little dove. You know that." He brushed his hand over her long hair over and over again. "Why do you want to go out in the ugly world when you can have everything you need or want right here?"

After months of indulging, Inayah became like a spoiled child, demanding more and more from him. "I want to go out." She stomped her silk slippered foot. "I want to go to a play or see a movie. I am tired of being held prisoner in these rooms!" She raised her voice and began to pace in front of him, back and forth, back and forth.

"I forbid it." He answered.

"Then I forbid you to make love to me." She raised her hand in the air, "I mean it. No more."

He watched her with some amusement, as she flipped her hand, her robe opened and he saw the sleek firm body he had come to love, peeking out. "Inayah, I can bring you movies to watch on the big screen." He pushed a button and a gigantic movie screen fell from the ceiling.

"I want to see people." Tears filled her eyes. "I want to go outside these walls."

He knew then that she was ready. He would give her an assignment and she would be grateful to have it. He felt he could finally trust her. "Okay. I want you to meet a man and I want you to bring him to me. Can you do that?"

She clapped her hands together as if she was the child he imagined her to be. "Yes, yes, I will do anything you ask."

"Then, after you bring him to me, I will reward you." He smiled.

She nodded.

"Good. Go and dress. Dress in your niqab. This man wants only women in niqab."

He saw her face droop. "I don't want to wear that."

"Inayah, you will do as I ask you to do." He shook his finger at her.

She nodded. "I will, but I don't want to." She exited into the bedroom, slamming the door behind her.

When she returned she was fully covered in her niqab and Abaya. Her eyes flashed behind the veil. "I hate this thing." She disputed.

He only retorted with, "Papa knows best." He reached out and drew her to him. "Baby, it is only because of this man and what he wants. Soon you can strip it off of you and wear your regular clothes." He paused, "Or no clothes." He laughed heartily at his own joke.

Inayah did not find him amusing. He hadn't given her the fix of cocaine that morning. He had purposely withheld it from her. She had begged, but he had told her she would only get some *candy* after she brought the gentleman to him.

"You must give it to me, George. I cannot think without it."

He smiled, "Candy is only for good little girls, Inayah. When you bring papa the man then you will be rewarded." He reached into his pocket. "Here is his picture." He handed the picture of the man to Inayah. "He is a man paid for by a sheik. The sheik wants only the best so bring me this man."

Inayah stared at the photo.

"You will meet him at the hotel and you will bring him here. I don't care how you manage it, but he must be here by tonight. Is that clear?" This voice was a different voice. She didn't understand George's abrupt tone.

"Why are you angry with me?" she asked.

"I am not angry, my little pet, but I don't want any mistakes. I have received a lot of money from the sheik for this little favor and it is important that you understand your mission."

She repeated, "Mission."

"Yes. This is your first mission as fis." He slapped her behind softly, "Family."

She moved toward the door. "How will I get to his hotel?"

"The limo driver will take you there. Remember, you must make no mistakes. I need this man here by tonight. I cannot emphasize the importance that you do that."

She nodded. "Okay. I will do it."

He reached out and pulled her towards him, "Say, I will do it for you, Papa." He wrapped her more tightly in his embrace.

"Papa."

"Oh, you know you melt my heart when you say that to me. Papa wants only the best for his little girl." He lifted her veil and pressed his lips tightly on hers. Then he growled, ominously, "Now, bring Papa the man."

She opened the door a crack and then slipped out into the hall. She remembered the way to the elevators, remembering that before, when she first arrived, there had been guards in the corridors, which were now empty. The elevator opened into an empty lobby. She expected to see George's guards at the reception desk, or even the familiar face of Shirley. There wasn't a soul to be seen. The barren scene unnerved her. She placed her hand on her thigh, feeling for her only friend, the one who gave her complete comfort. She felt the bulk of the knife and for a moment thought about pulling it out. She decided against it. She went to the revolving doors on the front of the building and walked to the curb where her limousine awaited.

"Madame." The driver opened the door for her. He stared away from her, not looking into her eyes.

He respects the niqab, she thought. *He has no clue as to who I am. Or maybe he does know.* She slid into the cold leather seat, as he slammed the door shut.

There was a wall separating her from the driver, so she looked out the windows as the driver drove down the New York streets. When the car stopped, he opened her door with as much dignity as he had previously. She politely said, "Thank you," when he offered his hand to help her out of the limo, but again, he never made eye contact with her. He motioned to the front of the building. It was a hotel, just as George had told her it would be. She walked up to the desk to ask for the man, but before she could speak the attendant said, "He is waiting for you. Seventh floor."

She stumbled for her voice, "W-what room?"

The attendant cocked his head in confusion, "The entire floor, madam."

She responded with an amazed, "Oh."

The elevator opened directly into a living room foyer. "Welcome, madam." A butler bowed and then led her into another room. "Inayah has arrived." He then disappeared back into the foyer.

A man dressed in a white Thobe turned toward her, "I have long waited for this meeting." He reached out and she offered her hand. He kissed the back of her hand softly. "Would you like a drink?"

Was this a test? She shook her head no, but she did not speak.

"Do you mind if I have one?"

She again shook her head.

"You have been out of circulation for a long time." He poured his drink, picked up and toasted her, "To your beauty that is held second to your mind."

She had heard this voice before. *Where have I heard that voice?* She thought. She rummaged through the compartments of her brain where she stored her childhood. *Ah, yes. My father's meetings. I know this voice, when I hid behind the chair, I remember this voice.*

"You can remove your veil if you wish." He offered, but she did not comply. "I want you to be comfortable." He smiled. "We are going to be spending a lot of time together."

She nodded, silently watching every movement of his hands and seeing the dark flash in his olive black eyes. She waited a moment, then decided to make her move before he became demanding. "I wish to go to my chambers to retrieve something. Will you go with me?"

He was surprised by her voice. "To your personal chambers?" The thought intrigued him.

"Yes." She whispered seductively, as she moved towards the door.

"Now?"

She nodded.

"Is it necessary? I also have very nice chambers." He motioned his entire arm towards the doors to his bedroom.

"I forgot something important." She whispered, as she blinked her eyes.

He placed his drink down on the round glass coffee table. "Ah. Now I understand. Alright then, we will go to your chambers. This time." He nodded his head as if he was granting her a boon. He pushed a button on his cell, "Edgar, bring the car around to the front. Madam and I are going back to her home." He smiled at Inayah. "Favors require payment."

She blinked her eyes. "Of course."

Once inside George's apartment building, everything happened quickly. Two very large muscular men grabbed the sheik from behind. He began to curse and scream, kicking his feet and turning his head back and forth. He kept shouting, "Bitch! Bitch!" She followed them to the elevator. His eyes were bulging with his anger. She moved to the farthest corner and stared at him as she thought of the *candy* that George had promised her. But George was nowhere to be seen.

She followed the men into a bare room, except for the one chair where they placed the man. They tied him to the chair and ripped his clothes to his waist. She moved to the rear of the room where a curtain hung separating a large table she hadn't seen before, from the rest of the room. She tightly gripped the edge of the sheer white curtain as she watched them place black sticky tape across the man's mouth before they left the room. She saw the man's eyes moving about the room. He pushed with his feet and raised the chair off the floor, but succeeded only in knocking himself and the chair to the floor. Now, he watched her from his prone position, kicking his bound feet in the air as he tried to right the chair. She kept her eyes on him. *Why had they left her in this room with this man? Where is George?* She let loose of the curtain and stood behind it, watching the man struggling on the floor. She heard the thump, thump, thump as he pounded his feet against the floor in his desperate attempts to free himself. He continued to struggle, rolling the chair back and forth, wriggling his shoulders up and down trying to loose the bindings on his wrists and around his shoulders. He began to bang his head against the floor. She shook her head slowly. *There's no escape.*

A door opened and a man in a white hospital coat entered. His mouth was covered with a surgical mask. "Stand the chair up!" he snapped at one of the guards, who immediately righted the man's chair. The masked man reached out and pushed back the man's hair as he placed his fingers on first one eye, widening it with his thumb and index finger and then did the same to the other. "No drugs?" He asked the guard. The guard shook his head. "Okay. Bring in the sterile plastic sheets."

The man in the chair began to bounce his feet on the floor and shake his head back and forth. She watched him with increasing interest. The guard came towards her and pulled back the curtain. She moved out of the way as he began to move the desk towards the center of the room. One of the guards carefully placed a white crisp plastic sheet on the table. The masked man ordered. "Place the chair on the table." The guard obliged and placed the man in the chair on his back on top of the table. The masked man ripped off the tape. "Do you have anything you want to say?"

"Why are you doing this to me?" the sheik's voice was high pitched and filled with panic.

The masked man nodded, "Of course you would want to know. You are of royal blood, correct?"

The sheik did not answer.

"Well, the fact of the matter is that we know that you are of royal blood. We need a transplant of..." he paused as if he was wondering if he should tell the man. "We need a heart of royal blood for a transplant."

The man in the chair began to wail, "Please, no, please! Don't do this. I have money, too. I have lots of money! Please don't do this! I'll pay higher than whatever they are paying you."

The man put a black toolbox on the table. "It isn't about money at this point, sir. It is about keeping an agreement. You could offer twice as much money and my client would still be served first. It is about honor. He needs a transplant from someone of royal blood. You can understand the urgency of this."

The man began to scream, but the man in the mask quickly replaced the tape on his mouth. Inayah stood back and watched through the curtain. A gush of air sucked into her lungs, as she realized what the masked man was about to do. She did not turn away, but saw the flash of a blade as he took the knife out of the toolbox. Her eyes widened in anticipation. She tried to look into the box to see what other tools the masked man had.

She stood on her tip toes, but couldn't see what else was in the box.

The masked man turned to one of the guards, "Go get the bowl with the liquid out of the operating room. Be sure not to touch the insides. I don't want any contamination."

The guard nodded.

Inayah watched as the masked man took a black marking pen from the box and began to mark on the man's chest. He spoke to his victim in a calm, unemotional tone. "We just need your heart, so you won't have to endure the kidneys first or the liver either for that matter. I have seen people suffer when I must do those first, but this will be quick. You appear healthy, so I am sure my client will be served well."

The man in the chair began to thrash wildly on the table.

"I would use anesthetic and make this easier for you, but we have none. An oversight, I assure you." He lifted the knife to the bright light above their heads, as he inspected it carefully. "I sharpened my tools last night. I take pride in that." Then, he turned towards Inayah. "You might want to come closer, madam. Watch and learn." He smiled. Inayah moved back behind the curtain and shook her head. The masked man laughed. "Suit yourself, but you may be required to obtain a heart one day yourself. At least if you watch you will be able to do this properly."

She did not move, but her breath puffed against the curtain, making the cloth move in and out against her lips with each of her breaths.

She imagined the man's screams as the knife cut into his chest. The blood spurted onto his chest and then onto the white plastic sheet. She didn't turn away, but heard the crunch of bone as the knife stabbed into the heaving chest, and then she watched in fascination as the masked man lifted the heart gently from the chest and placed it in the solution in the bowl. The man in the chair did not move again. The guards wheeled a green trash can into the room and slid the man's body, the sheet, and the chair into the hard plastic can. They placed the lid on, after some shoving and pushing. Then they wheeled the trash can out of the room. The man in the mask followed them with the bowl containing the heart held tightly in his hands. The door was left wide open. Dazed, she walked into the hall. They had all disappeared into the elevator. She looked back at the open door. With gentle footsteps she returned to the door and closed it softly. Then, as an after-thought, she reopened the door and slid her hand in around the corner to shut the lights. She closed the door again and made her way to the elevator. She pushed the button for the seventh floor. *George better have her candy ready after all this!*

She opened the door to the suite. George was not there. She hurried into the bedroom to see if he had left the cocaine on the wardrobe table. He had not. Her heart jumped. She began to breathe heavily. Her head and stomach ached. *Where are you George?* She wiped her dripping nose with a tissue as she whispered, "Oh no, he's made me an addict. I need it!" She turned her body in a circle and continued to spin until she fell on the floor. "George! George! Papa where is my candy?" Tears streaked her cheeks. She went to the windows over-looking the streets below.

She heard a loud bang in the living room and quickly ran to the bedroom door. When she opened it she saw George with his arms around a man who was wrapped in rope from is neck to his feet. George looked up when he saw her and released his grip on the man's chest. "Oh, it's you Inayah. Say hello to Mohammed."

She didn't speak, but watched as George threw the man onto the couch. "I've ordered a plastic sheet." He didn't look up, but she knew, since no one else was in the room, George was speaking only to her. Since she had just seen a man lose his heart on a plastic sheet, she knew that this man was going to have some kind of similar fate. Her heart began to quicken with excitement.

"For the last time, Enrique, where is the shipment going to take place?" The man on the couch continued to look at his bridled hands, but he did not speak. "Inayah, roll out the plastic sheet."

She did as she was asked. George directed the man to the middle of the plastic sheeting. He checked to make sure all the rope bindings were tight.

Then he handed an ice pick to Inayah. "Find out where the shipment is coming in. I will be taking a bath." He plopped the ice pick in her hand and then he left her alone with the man.

She studied the man for a few moments. He was dressed in jeans and a pull over shirt, certainly not rich like the last man she had seen murdered earlier in the day. She rolled the ice pick in her hand, feeling the solid oak handle conform to her hand. "There is no reason to die," she whispered softly.

The man shouted, "You bitch! You whore!"

She shook her head and clicked her tongue, "No, now that isn't nice at all." She went into the kitchen and returned with a dish cloth. She shoved it into his mouth. "There we go. I will only take it out if you nod your head yes to me, is that clear?" The man thrashed his body on the sheeting. "Now, we need to know where the shipment is coming." She thought about it a moment. *Was that why she had no candy? He was withholding where the candy was!* As soon as the thought crossed her mind she slowly began to push the ice pick into the man's thigh, slowly and deliberately, twisting it as she pushed it in. She saw the agony in the man's eyes. "Oh, does that hurt? Are you going to tell me where the shipment is coming in?" He did not nod his head. She yanked out the ice pick and placed it against his cheek. "I once saw a man in a circus pull a cloth through his cheek. Have you seen that? " She began to push the point into his cheek as she saw his feet bouncing up and down with his pain. A slow smile crossed her lips and one corner of her mouth lifted up in a sneer. "Hurts?" She pushed and sent the ice pick through his mouth and tongue and out his other cheek. Tears filled the man's eyes. She laughed. "Well, look at that. Now you can pull a scarf through one side to the other. I dare say I hit your tongue didn't I?" She pulled down her veil and tossed her hair into the man's face. "So, where is the shipment going to be? A woman needs her candy." She laughed softly. The man did not nod his head.

She rushed to his feet and removed one tennis shoe. "Let's see if you are ticklish." She slid the point of the ice pick from the ball of his foot to his heel, but she did not cut through the skin. He tried to move his feet away and then she jabbed the pick through his ankle into the floor. "Oops. I hope he won't get upset with me for making a hole in the floor." The man had arched his back in pain and banged his head on the floor. "So, where's the shipment coming in?" She yanked the ice pick out of his ankle and watched the blood oozing onto the plastic sheet. The man began to nod. "Good.

Good." She reached for his mouth and withdrew the dish cloth.

"Warehouse on the water." His voice was jagged and heavy with his pain.

"Which warehouse?" She asked.

"By the transit center where you catch the ferry to Jersey."

She shook her head. "Not good enough. There are a lot of warehouses down there. Do you have an address?"

He shook his head.

She rested the ice pick on his stomach. "Okay. I am going to count to three and then I am going to make a peep hole into your tummy." She grinned. "My guess is that this ice pick will cause quite a bit of damage in there. I mean, it's not like your cheek or your ankle."

"Lady, I don't know. Truly, I don't know the address. I just drive there and find it. That's it."

She pushed gently on the handle of the ice pick and watched a small trickle of blood go down the sides of his very white stomach. He began to scream in a high-pitched voice which reminded her of a girl's scream. She shoved the cloth in his mouth. "You don't want to disturb his nice bath now, do you?" She watched his brows raise and fall and his eyes squinting with the pain. "So, could you describe exactly how I could drive there? I mean, exactly?"

He nodded.

"Okay. Good. I will ask George if that is a possibility." She smiled at him. "Wait right here." She went to the bedroom door and called in, " Can he guide you there in the car, George?"

George grumbled, "Yeah sure. I'll have one of my guys take him. I just need to know the place, that's all." She heard the bathtub's water sloshing with his movement.

She returned to the man on the white sheet which was now speckled with spots of blood and a small pool had formed under the man's ankle and under his thigh. "Okay, he says you can just show one of the guys. They will follow your directions to the spot. See, that was easy, wasn't it? I just wish you had told me before we had to do all this." She turned her palms up and moved her hands outward toward his head and feet. "Don't you feel better now?" She asked sweetly.

She heard him growl within his throat.

She lifted the ice pick and glanced at his pants, where his private parts were hidden from view. As if he had read her thoughts, he tried to turn on his side. She slid the point of the ice pick an inch under his waistband. "You better take the guard to the right place, is that clear?"

He nodded.

She laughed softly. "I wish I had started here." She slipped her veil back over her face.

She then walked to the front door and called the guard. "Take this man for a ride. He will show you where the shipment is coming in. Then bring him back here. We are not quite done talking." Her smile did not light up her eyes.

"Yes, m'am." The guard glanced behind her at the man on the white sheeting. "Shall I just have him carried out on the sheet?"

She nodded. "No use letting him drip blood all the way down in the elevator."

"I'll take him out the basement." The guard went to the sheet and wrapped the thrashing man tightly and then dragged the sheet to the elevator. She watched as the guard pulled the man onto the elevator. Satisfied that everything was going well, she turned to go back into the apartment. She glanced down at her niqab and noticed a blotch of blood right in the middle of the front. She sighed, "Work means getting dirty sometimes." She grinned. She went into the bedroom, removed the niqab and went naked into the bathroom. "May I join you, Papa?" she asked.

George patted the rise of bubbles. "Sure baby, right here." The water splashed with his patting, as she eased herself into the tub. "Everything alright, baby?"

She nodded. "Papa, did you bring me candy?"

"Sorry honey, we have to wait for the shipment."

She felt her eye twitching.

Chapter 11

"There's someone I want you to meet, sweetie." George sipped his tea from his favorite rose printed tea cup. She was sitting on the white couch with her legs curled under her, reading her magazine. She looked up quickly.

"Who?"

"His name is John. He's a nice man and he asked me for a very special night. I thought you would like to give him that night for me." His voice twined and twisted through the air like a deceptive snake. He hadn't asked her to go out with other men for months. Sometimes she had to sleep with them if she wanted her *candy* when she returned to the apartment. Lately, she was using less, trying to get off the habit, but then she would sweat and shake and her entire body would be racked with pain. Sometimes she went into the bedroom and rolled on the bed with her agony, but she didn't tell him that she was trying to come off the cocaine. She didn't know what he would do to her. She stared at him holding his teacup with both of his hands in front of his face.

"I don't feel like meeting anyone." She answered in a clear voice.

"What do you mean, baby? This guy is not like regular New Yorkers. He's from upstate and sweet.

He wants to take you to a play, this and nothing more." George smiled at her.

"I don't want to go out with anyone, George. Please don't make me."

"Go get dressed, sweetie. Put on that beautiful black dress that clings to your curves. I love seeing you in that." He licked his lips. "You do this for Papa and I will give you some nice candy, the best, when you get back." He winked his eye.

The cocaine did not motivate her. She was almost done with it. She wanted her head clear and the pollution out of her body. She whipped her hair to the front of her body. "Okay. I'll go." She got slowly off the couch and slapped her magazine on the table. She went into the bedroom and locked the door. She knew he had a key, but she also knew he heard her do it and it would make him angry. He would know she wasn't happy and for some reason when she wasn't happy, George wasn't happy.

He tapped on the door. "Sweetie, don't shut Papa out. Open the door my little bird." He tapped again. She pressed her head against the closed door. Her thoughts drowned her, *I want to get out of here. I want my life back.* He tapped gently again. "Please sweetie, open the door. Papa doesn't want to have to use his key."

She turned the lock and slowly opened the door. "What do you want?" She asked as she looked up into his eyes.

"I want you, my sweet little girl. I want you right now." He took her by the hand and began to walk her to the bed. He slapped his hand hard on her firm little butt. "Papa wants his baby right now." He pushed her on to the bed. "Then you can go to see the play with John."

John was pleasantly surprised when Inayah's legs swung out of the black limousine. He reached out to help her. He felt the warmth of her fingertips in his hand and his eyes stared into her dark eyes.

"I'm Inayah." She whispered.

"I'm Lawrence."

She jerked her head, as if he had thrown cold water on her. "Are you the man I am supposed to meet for the play?"

He nodded. "Sometimes my friends call me Larry, but I prefer, Lawrence. My mother named me after her father."

She repeated his name, "Lawrence. I like that name, too." *Why had George called him John?* she wondered.

He wrapped his arm around her as he guided her into the theater. He presented his two tickets as they walked in. "Do you like plays?"

She didn't know if she should tell him that this was her first play. Would he think she was nothing but a backwards bedroom whore? She glanced up at the old billboards on the theater's red and gold velvet walls. "Oh yes. I've seen Annie and Le Miserable."

"Well, I think you are going to love tonight's play!" He announced with obvious pleasure. "We are going to see the musical, *Wicked*. Have you seen it?"

She shook her head.

"Wonderful! Let's get in our seats, uh, unless you need to use the powder room."

"I'm fine, thank you." He put his arm through hers and walked her to their seats. They were perfect, giving them a view of the entire stage. She felt her stomach swoon with excitement. She never dreamed a room could be so elegant. She watched as people found their seats and let the activity in the huge auditorium wash over her. He placed his hand on hers, "You are very pretty, Inayah."

She looked into his brown eyes. She knew he expected her to talk to him, but she didn't know what she should say. "Where are you from?" she asked.

"Oh, it's a small town way out in the boonies. Nothing much ever happens there." He paused, "Although, a year or so back we had a double murder."

He got a faraway look in his eyes, as if he was seeing the murder scene. "I'm a police chief." He offered. "Hope that doesn't bother you."

Silently she shook her head, no.

"Yeah, we had this double murder. A man and his daughter's betrothed. They were Muslims and we also had this other Muslim guy killed. Found his head in a fireplace." He paused, "Am I grossing you out?"

Her mouth opened to a perfect "O". She felt her brow begin to bead with glistening beads. "It's just warm in here."

He smiled warmly, "I did gross you out. I am so sorry. I don't know what got into me. I never talk about cases, especially with a pretty girl sitting next to me."

"I'm okay, really. Did you catch the murderer?"

"No, can't say that I did. Wish I could say so, but nope. The thing is, we figured out that the daughter had been up in this farmhouse with the boyfriend, but she must've run away before the father got there." He scratched his head, "What always bugs me is that there was this other murder at the bus station. I mean they probably all aren't related." He looked into her eyes, "What do you think?"

She sat very still. "I-I don't know. I would have to have more facts."

He chuckled. "Why, you'd be a great detective, wanting all the facts before you make a determination. I like that!"

The music started rising from the orchestra pit. He turned towards the curtains, but she continued to stare at him. The knife under her dress made its presence known, as it pressed deeply into her thigh. Just before the curtains opened, she asked, "Where did you meet George?"

"Oh, I knew of him through a friend of a friend. I paid top dollar so I knew that he would find me the perfect date, and he did!" He suddenly bent towards her and kissed her cheek. "You are perfect!" He then turned towards the stage, but held her hand tightly in his, squeezing it every now and again.

Her thoughts raced. Does he know? Does he know who I am? I used my real name? Does he know the name of the daughter? Of course he would! He knows. He knows! She looked at his hand holding hers so tightly. I will wait until intermission and then I will go to the restroom.

She immediately thought differently, No, he will follow me if it is intermission. She leaned towards him, "Lawrence, I need to use the lady's room."

"Oh, of course." He whispered. He stood and allowed her to pass in front of him. "I'll be right here waiting." He winked at her and sat back down.

She hurried up the center aisle. She walked through the lobby and ran out into the street. "Taxi! Taxi!" She called out, raising her hand in which she held a small black clutch-purse. A yellow cab slid into a stop in front of her. She grabbed the door handle and snapped out her order, "Grand Central." She plopped into the backseat. She closed her eyes for a moment. *James is alive.* The thought brought tears to her eyes. *Alive.* She wrapped her arms tightly around her shoulders.

Grand Central Station was packed with people. The Station was a perfect place for her to blend in. There were concert goers, late night dinner dates, business men and women finally leaving their office. She bought her ticket, grateful that she had thought enough to skim a little every day from George's wallet on top of the dresser. She had been taking fives and tens for months. She smiled inwardly at her cleverness.

She sat near the window on the train, leaning her head against the cool glass. *What if he doesn't want me now? It's been a long time. What if he has someone else?* Her thoughts tortured her. She closed her eyes, not wanting to sleep, but to just rest her mind. Sleep came anyway and plunged her into snippets of the past—her Aunt Mahibah's face, smiling, her father beating her, while she rolled into a ball in the kitchen, the feel of the steel hanger in her tightly clutched hand, the eyes of the man as she plunged the ice pick into his body. Her eyes popped open. *Enough!*

She stared emotionless out the window at the industrial buildings passing by the window. She kept her gaze steady as farms whizzed by, with dairy cows watching the train, chewing their cud. The world seemed to stand still and only she was moving through it. The train slowed as it came to the destination. She stood and smoothed her little black dress with her hand. She knew she would have to find different clothes as soon as possible. Lawrence would be seeking the woman in the little black dress. She thought, *I will find a Muslim community, steal an Abaya and niqab and hide among them until it is safe.* But her second thought was, *I have no idea where that Muslim stronghold is!* As if an answer to a silent prayer, she looked up and saw a man and woman dressed in Arab attire. The man was in his Thobe and the woman covered with her niqab and Abaya. Inayah followed them on silent, soft, furtive footsteps. She stayed in the shadows, moving stealthly into the building storefronts to hide in her clandestine effort to stay concealed from the Arab couple's view.

The Muslim couple walked for blocks and blocks. She kept up with their pace, even though she was wearing her high heels. Her steps were so muted and guarded, her prey never knew that she was following them. When they stopped in front of an apartment building, she quickly concealed herself behind a wall. She glanced at the other people walking on the sidewalk, most were in their Arab clothes. They glanced towards her hiding place, as she pretended to look in the store windows. She watched the man unlock the door and the two unsuspecting victims disappeared into the building. She then kept walking past their door, turned down an alley, keeping her eyes peeled for a clothesline that might be laden with drying niqab and Abaya. She found only one such clothesline and all it had blowing in the night breezes was a pair of black socks. She kept walking until she came to the back of the apartments. Trashcans were lined up neatly, some with their lids secure, others with their lids askew inviting the rats of the neighborhood to have their pick of their dinner delights. She jumped when she heard a man's voice behind her.

"New to the neighborhood?" The voice asked in a tone that could only be explained as, amused.

She placed her hand on her hip and felt the familiar bulge. She glared at the man with a bag of trash clutched in front of him. He was dressed in blue jeans, his brown hair appeared as if he hadn't combed it for weeks. The one thing she made note of instantly was that he was not of Arab descent.

She nodded, "I'm lost."

He laughed, "Well, I guess so! You are dressed to the nines and walking in an alley next to the trashcans. I'd say that is REALLY lost." He chuckled again as he tossed the bag of trash into one of the cans and then he took the time to make sure the lid was secured. "Damn rats around her are as big as cats."

Her hand relaxed against her leg. "So you live here?" She asked.

"Yep. Lucky me." He laughed again. "And you?"

"Like I said, I'm lost. I got off at the wrong station and started walking before I realized where I was." She lied.

"That happens in the dark." He stared at her bare legs, her shoes, and then his eyes traversed her body until he looked into her eyes. "Women around here don't usually go out alone after dark. You landed in a Muslim community."

She nodded, "It would seem so. I am looking for the Mosque or perhaps a kindly woman to take me in for the night." Another lie.

He seemed undaunted by her words. "Well, yes, that probably is a solution." He paused, "Or you could come home with me. I usually collect stray dogs and cats and an occasional human being, but they certainly don't look as together as you are." He grinned. "Maybe you should just get a taxi and go back to the station."

She considered his words, but knew that the station would be exactly where Lawrence would look for her. He would never look for her in this man's apartment. "I'm Sally." She announced with firm conviction.

"I'm Tom." He offered his hand, but she didn't take it. "I'm really a nice guy. I live here so that I can be near the university. I'm a teacher. I don't like having to drive on the God-awful freeways to work each morning, so I live in this cheap neighborhood near the school and walk to work. Nice arrangement if you can get it."

She didn't smile back, but then realized that he expected a smile, so she gave him one. "Well, maybe I could take a taxi to a hotel near here."

He shook his head. "Nope. No hotels for about fifteen miles. I'm your best offer." He grinned again. "I think it's a descent offer, considering that I am offering my home to you and I have NO clue as to who you are and where you came from."

She quickly said, "Yes, of course, you are being very friendly and accommodating."

He interjected, "And you are wondering why is this guy being so nice?" He nodded, "Of course, naturally you would ask yourself that, heck, I'm asking myself that. I just came out to dump my trash. I didn't say, oh, I think I'll go pick up some woman who is walking among the trashcans."

She looked down, he was right. Instantly, she let down her guard and smiled at him, a genuinely relaxed and off-guard smile. "I'm sorry. It's just that it is late and dark and I'm so confused and lost and..."

He took a step towards her, "Look Sally, I think you should come with me to my apartment, have a soothing cup of tea and we will get you a taxi back to a hotel. I promise I won't bite you or harm you in any way."

"What do you teach?" she asked out of the blue.

"I teach history. So, is that a yes? A rather disguised yes, but a yes?"

She nodded.

"Good. Come on. Let's get out of Rat City and you will feel much better." She followed him, her eyes were no longer looking left and right with suspicion and caution. He pointed to a door, "We go through this and then down to my basement apartment. See my window down there." He pointed to a well that had a window. "I told you places are cheap here and I got one of the cheapest, but it's nice enough."

She didn't speak, but followed him in the door and down the stairwell to his apartment door. He fiddled with his keys and opened the green door. "Home sweet home." He turned to look at her, "Welcome!" He hurried in leaving her at the door. He quickly put a kettle of water on the stove and then turned to see her still standing in the entry. "Sally, come on in. It's okay. We'll have some tea and then we can talk a bit and get you a taxi."

Her eyes scanned the room before she sat on the small leather couch. Several multi-colored pillows were placed against each other on the couch. She saw two more doors off what she supposed was the living room. As if he read her mind, he pointed to each door, "My bedroom and bathroom."

"May I use your bathroom?" She asked.

"Of course! Mi casa, su casa!" He reached up into a cupboard and she saw boxes of tea, all with their labels facing the same way. He grabbed one of them and zipped open two small packets. He dangled a tea bag into a pink mug and another one into a yellow mug. "You go on in. It's clean." He smiled.

The bathroom was exactly as he stated, impeccably clean. She used her finger to slowly open the medicine cabinet, just to see what he had inside it. Everything was neatly placed, with labels plainly seen. Bandages, hair tonic, toothpaste. All items were lined up, with their corners touching. She looked down at the sink, expecting to find a loose hair, or a dribble of old toothpaste, but the sink sparkled. Even the chrome spout was shiny, with not even one drip of water stain on it. She slid the flowered shower curtain back to reveal the tub and shower. The quick reveal was of a glistening white tub, large white bar of soap, a caddy hanging from the neck of the shower nozzle with shampoo and cream rinse. *Tom is a very neat guy.* She lifted the lid of the toilet and stared into the pristine white bowl. She scrunched up her dress to her hips, pulled down her lace black panties and plopped her white bottom on the sanitized toilet seat. She shook her head, *I have never seen such a clean bathroom!* She looked down at her feet, which were planted firmly on polished white tiles. "Too much," She said aloud.

After she washed her hands and wiped them on the white hand towel, she used the towel to rub down the faucet, making sure all the drips of water were gone. She opened the door and saw that Tom had put a small teapot on the coffee table on a black tray. She saw two teacups and two teaspoons.

"Your tea is ready to pour." He moved towards her and she stopped. She looked at his face. *What is it about this guy?* She asked herself. His face was kind and his manner gentle, but there was something that she could not quite put her finger on. She was bothered by his solicitous attitude. *Tom is too kind*. She told herself.

"Look, Sally, I need to get to bed because 6 a.m. comes up really fast. Why don't I get you a blanket and some sheets and you can sleep on the couch tonight. Then tomorrow you can get an early start to where ever you are going."

Her head was spinning with her thoughts. It was logical that she should lay low for the night. Lawrence would be looking for her. He would be asking questions at the train station and he would be walking the streets, not to mention that George would have his men looking for her. She nodded, "Okay, yes. I will take you up on that offer. It is late and I don't know where I could find a hotel."

He nodded with smug satisfaction. He disappeared into his bedroom and then came out with his arms full of blankets, sheets, and a pillow. "I wish I had a bed for you, but the couch isn't too uncomfortable. I'd give you my bed, but..." he paused.

"No, you are doing more than enough. I don't even know why you are helping me."

He chuckled, "You have an aura about you that I find fascinating, if that makes any sense to you. I mean, it's not every day I meet a well-dressed woman standing amidst my trash cans."

She was speechless as she watched him making her bed. He patted the pillow, "There you go. See you in the morning. Coffee or tea?"

"What?"

"In the morning, coffee or tea?" he asked again. "Breakfast?"

"Coffee, no breakfast." She answered stupefied.

"Okay, but breakfast is the most important meal of the day." He grinned.

"Tom, I don't know how to thank you," she shook her head.

"Oh! One more thing." He hurried out the room and returned with a blue pair of pajamas. "Mine, of course; they will be a little big, but I think they'll do." He held the blue pajamas out in front of him. "See you in the morning."

She started to speak, but he had already disappeared behind his bedroom door. She went into the bathroom to dress for bed. She slept quite well, only opening her eyes once when she heard a dog barking in the street. The sun came through the top of the windows and lit up the kitchen.

"Good morning, Sally!" Tom came out of his bedroom with his arms full of clothes and hurried to the bathroom. She didn't even have enough time to greet him back. When he came back out, he was fully dressed.

They heard a sharp knock on the apartment door.

She jumped behind the couch, fell to her knees and hid.

"It's just the door. Might be my friend, Darrell." His lips turned up in an amused smile. "You're okay. This neighborhood isn't THAT bad." He laughed as he opened the door. "Hello!" he said when he saw the man standing at the door.

"Hey, Tom, are you going to work today or not? I was waiting on the street corner and man, it's getting late."

"I'm sorry, Darrell. Yes, I'm going, but you should go on ahead and walk without me." He slapped his friend's shoulder. "I have a guest and I want to make sure she is okay."

"She? You got a she in here?" Darrel laughed.

"I do. She's lost and I'm helping her."

Darrell laughed again as he tried to look around Tom's body that was blocking his vision of the apartment.

Inayah stayed behind the couch, listening to their conversation. She was grateful when the door finally closed. She stood up slowly. "So, that's your friend, Darrel."

"He's a teacher, too." He stopped and looked at her trying to judge what her response might be, "He's also my boyfriend."

Ah, now it all made perfect sense. Now she knew that she had been correct in her assumption about Tom. No wonder he was so nice. She felt her body tension begin to leave. Tom really is gay. Tom-the-gay-man is quite amazing, she thought, as she glanced at the car keys hanging on the hook.

She thought of the irony of a gay man living in an Arabic enclave. "So Tom, do you have a car?" She asked quickly, changing the subject.

"I do. I park it in the lot behind the apartments. A Honda Accord. Fire engine red." He chuckled. "Do you need me to drive you somewhere?" He reached for a hook on the wall that had several keys hanging on it.

She shook her head, "No. I'm just going to walk back to the train station and get back on track after you go to work."

"Okay. Well, do you mine locking up because I have to get rolling?"

She laid her hand on the knife at her side, hidden under Tom's pajama bottoms. She watched Tom gather some books and then saw him stand in front of the door, with his hand poised on the knob. "I guess I probably won't see you again." He said sadly.

She wondered why his voice was so sad. He barely knew her. She looked into his eyes and released her hand from her thigh. "Good bye, Tom. Thank you."

He chuckled, that warm chuckle that disarmed her every time she heard it. "Good bye, Sally." The door closed. She hurried to the bathroom and then, as an after-thought, ran into his bedroom and pulled out a pair of jeans and a shirt. She thought of scribbling him a thank you note, but thought better of it. She tied her hair into a bun on top of her head.

She snatched the keys off the hook and hurried out the door, locking it securely behind her. She ran to the parking lot behind the apartments and looked for the red Honda Accord. She clicked the button on the key and heard a loud honking horn. She slid into the seat, turned the ignition on and looked at the gas gauge. She knew that it would be a full tank and it was. Tom was one dependable guy. She whispered, "I'm glad I didn't kill you, Tom." Of course, she knew that he had no idea how closely he came to death last night.

She followed the road signs and before she knew it, she was in familiar territory. The grandfather's farmhouse was only minutes away. Her thoughts plagued her, *Perhaps James wouldn't be there. Maybe he sold the home after the murders.* She watched as the familiar forest closed in around the road and obstructed her view. She stared into the woods and saw only more trees. Then, in a clearing, filled with the stumps of dying trees, she saw someone with an axe.. He was swinging the axe high in the air and bringing it down on the stumps, splitting them in half. She stopped the car as the man turned to look in her direction. He put his hand over his eyes. The man's hair was long, touching his shoulders, bouncing in bushy curls, as his axe hit the wood. His dark beard fluffed around his face. His stare intensified, as he continued to watch her.

Then, satisfied that he didn't know who she was, he turned his back and began to chop again at another stump , but she continued to watch him. She knew that back, those legs in that stance, she knew those eyes. She turned off the ignition, popped open her door and stood next to the front fender, watching him chop at the log. He must have felt her eyes on him. He turned slowly and saw her standing next to the car. He turned his head one way and then the other, squeezing one of his eyes to give him a clearer view. Unexpectedly, the axe fell from his hands...

Chapter 12

Love often blooms on seemingly hard unyielding ground, like a flower blossoming between two rocks. The love of Inayah and James was no less resilient than a flower on a rocky slope. He couldn't believe that he had her in his arms again. For a while they flourished in perfect days of love-making from sunrise to sunset and beyond. James didn't ask her where she had been or how she had lived. He dove into the depths of her eyes and became lost in the essence of her. Nothing else mattered, only her love. She, in turn, made sure that the padlocks were on the dossiers of her brain where hidden atrocities abided. She allowed herself the joy of his deep kisses, the caresses of his warm gentle hands, the safety of his strong arms. No memories were allowed to surface, only the *now*, here with him, bathed in his love.

She giggled softly as he nibbled on her ear and kissed the line of her jaw. "I love you, James," she whispered. He folded her naked body closer to his and held her even more tightly.

"I love you, too, my darling. Are you happy?" He asked.

She wished he hadn't asked her. She wished he had just let the moments roll into each other without any thoughts, but he had asked and now she had to answer. She knew the answer he wanted, but now, she examined her conscience and realized that, no, she was not happy. There was a world that she had been a part of and she wanted that world. It was a world of power and she had been on the brink of acquiring that power. "I," she began and then stopped, not knowing how to explain to him that she needed more. Immediately, she examined her mind and asked herself, *why isn't this enough? Why do I have to spoil this perfect joy?* But she knew why. She had a thirst for something that he would never understand. She didn't even totally understand her desires. She looked deeply into his eyes and kissed his mouth softly. She ventured, "I want to go back to New York."

He thoughtfully looked into her eyes. "I see. So, this farm life is too quiet for you." He nodded trying to conceal his hurt. The realization that he was not enough for her stung him. "Okay, so we will go to New York." He managed to smile. "I want you to be happy, darling. If you like the bright lights and the excitement of New York, then so be it. We will go to New York." He knew that he could refuse nothing that she wanted. Now he had her back in his life and he would never let go of her! "I love you my sweet and I want you always to be happy. If New York makes you happy, then we will get an apartment in New York and live there. I don't care. I just want to be with you."

Her eyes blinked and she said, "I have an apartment. We can go there."

He tried to hide the surprise in his voice, but his "Oh," came out of his mouth dripping with his shock. "I didn't know you still had an apartment. Okay. We will go there."

She sat up quickly and spoke with excited anticipation, "You will love it, James. The apartment has lots of windows that overlook the city and you can see so far! There are stores close by and a park and there is so much to do there." She was rattling on like an excited child. He loved to see her eyes sparkle with her excitement.

"Sounds lovely." He managed to say, in spite of the ache he suddenly felt in his heart. The realization that he was no longer enough for her, that the farm wasn't enough, that the peaceful existence of everyday life was not enough, pained him somehow. He thought that they would have their children here on the farm, that they would become a family. But as he watched her hands suddenly become animated with her speech and he saw the sparks ignite in her eyes, he knew that the farm was not where she would be happy. He would do anything to make her happy. He reached out and pulled a strand of her hair from her eyes. "Darling, we will go wherever makes you happy. I just want you to be happy."

She snuggled against him. Now her world would be perfect. She would have James and she would have the power she so urgently craved. She would have it all.

"We'll go tomorrow." He said with finality.

She shook her head, "I'll go ahead and get things ready for us. I want to clean up before you see it. Then, in a few days you can join me." She hadn't asked what he thought or asked for his opinion.

"I thought we'd go together. I can help you clean up and..."

She shook her head. "No, I want to do it myself. I want it to be all clean and sparkling fresh for you before you see it. Oh, James, you understand, don't you darling?"

Her childlike insistence melted his heart. "Whatever you want, my darling. Okay. I will join you in a few days when you tell me that all has been spruced up to your liking." He laughed. "A little mess certainly isn't going to bother me. I don't really care what kind of housekeeper you are. We would clean it together, but if this is what you want, then so be it."

She smiled with smug satisfaction. "I will pack and go then. Can you drop me at the train station?"

He nodded, but even as he agreed to her wishes, his heart sank at the thought of being without her again. "You will be careful, won't you darling? New York is a big city and..."

She hugged him tightly, "Don't worry about a thing, my sweet. You are going to love the apartment and you know what, maybe we can go from New York to the farm and back and forth. What do you think of that idea?"

"I like it! Yes, we can have some city life and then when we need a break we can come out here to the back woods." He laughed warmly, "Perfect, Inayah. You have it all figured out, don't you?"

She smiled sweetly, "I do. When the city is too hot, we can cool off in the country life."

While he was thinking of the summer heat of New York, she had *other* types of *heat* on her mind. Her mind was racing with her thoughts and plans. Her biggest obstacle was, *What to do about George?* She knew immediately what she must do, of course, but for her the problem was *how* to do what needed to be done. She felt her eye begin to twitch. She unconsciously put her hand to her cheek.

Chapter 13

The niqab blew in the wind. The cold blast of winter stung her eyes as she walked along the New York sidewalk. She nodded to the doorman as she jingled her key out in front of her for him to see that yes, she belonged there. She went to the elevator and nodded to the guard stationed there, and again, showed the keychain with the gold star plainly visible. She punched at the button of the elevator, feeling the rush of adrenaline in her blood. She threw her head back and let the excitement wash over her. The knife strapped to her leg seemed to scream at her for attention. She reached down and patted it gently, like an owner patting a faithful dog.

The elevator opened onto the foyer with the familiar double doors. She looked left and right, but saw no one. *Amazing,* she thought. *All those guards, but none right here.* Her immediate thought was *why?* She placed her key in the lock, stepped to the side of the door and kicked the door open.

She saw him sitting there, with a white chair posed to face the entry doors. He had a gun across his knees and he was looking right into her eyes. "Hello, Inayah. I have been waiting for you." George smiled, a tight-lipped grin.

The air sucked into her lungs and then she smiled at him, but he could only see her eyes with her niqab obstructing her smile. "Hello, George."

"You didn't bring the boyfriend?" He asked with almost a whine to his voice.

"There is no boyfriend, George."

He pointed the gun at her, "Really? I think I know better." He stood slowly, but continued to point the gun at her. "James, isn't it?"

She was silent.

"Yes, that's his name, James. You lost no time in finding him and then you stayed with him." His voice was almost a growl. "You slept with him."

"He means nothing, George. A mere pawn." She flipped her hand in the air.

George kept the gun steadily on her. "My informants tell me differently. Seems you went on a killing spree." He grinned. "Does Papa's apple not fall far from the tree?"

She felt the knife shouting its presence and her heart began to race. Would she be able to remove the knife fast enough before he shot her? "It's not what you think, George. I was setting him up, I..."

"Do you know how long I waited for you to return? Of course not. You didn't even think of me here waiting, did you?" He placed the tip of the gun under her chin. Then, keeping the gun aimed at her head he walked around her slowly, like a lion stalking his prey. "I waited, Inayah. For days." His final steps brought him directly in front of her. He stopped and stared into her eyes. "Days, Inayah."

She whispered, "I'm sorry, George."

He slowly lowered the gun, just inches, just mere moments. In those moments she brought her knife up and stabbed him through her gown into his stomach. Then she hit the gun, knocking it toward the ceiling, as he pulled the trigger. The bullet shot a hole in the ceiling. She grabbed for the gun as his hands released their grip. He fell back, with his hands over the wound. "Inayah," he whispered. His eyes filled with tears.

"Yes, George. You have something to tell me."

"I would have," he moaned, "I would have given you everything. Anything..." He began to cough. "Why?" He fell against the glass coffee table. She kept her eyes steadily on him.

"I don't need you to give me anything, George. If I want it, I take it. I am taking over now." She smiled. "Thank you for that."

His blood continued to gush onto the table, over the palms of his hands. "Help me, Inayah."

She took her foot and pushed his chest, forcing him onto the floor. She heard the knock at the door. "Come in." She said sweetly. Three armed men rushed in. She shot a bullet into each chest before they could even aim their guns at her. She stood over one of them, with the gun pointed at his face, "Tell me how many more of you? Hurry."

"Maybe ten." He gurgled.

"Ten?" She put her foot on his chest. "For sure, ten? Talk to me!" She pushed her foot harder into his chest.

"Maybe twelve." He began to breathe heavily as his blood filled his lungs. "Please, call an ambulance."

"Sure." She said, as she pulled the trigger once again, killing him.

Inayah hurried to the open door and slipped out into the hallway. She could hear the elevator moving up. She moved into the shadows with the gun's barrel pointed toward the elevator doors. Unexpectedly, eight men screamed, "Don't shoot!" Their hands were in the air. "You are the Kyre! You are Kyre!" They chanted that she was the boss. "You are Kyre of this fis." One of them stepped toward her. She started to squeeze the trigger, "No, don't do it! We will follow you. All of us."

Her eyes glared out at all of them. She scanned their bodies from their heads to their feet. None of them were carrying a gun. "Face down on the floor." She kicked her foot at the one who had pronounced her the Kyre. "You, take off your clothes."

"What?" He asked.

"Take off your clothes." She ordered.

He began to wiggle out of his jacket and then his pants.

"Stand up." She ordered. He stood before her in his under shorts. "Now all of you, do the same."

The other seven men quickly took off their clothes and stood before her in their underwear. She nodded. "Okay. You all proclaim me Kyre?" She asked. They nodded vigorously. She laughed, "I am the Kyre who leads semi-naked men." She kept laughing. "Okay, we will continue business as usual. We will operate under Besa, until I cannot trust you any longer. Is that clear?" The men nodded. "George is dead. You," she pointed to the man who had first proclaimed her Kyre, "You will be Kyetar. I will rely on you as my underboss. Your first mission is to order this mess cleaned up. Who can I trust to guard my door?"

The man nodded, "Any of us, my Kyre." Her eyes slowly scanned them again. "Okay, you," she pointed to another man. "You will guard my door. Kill anyone who approaches without clearance, is that clear?"

"Yes."

"You," She pointed her gun at the man, "Get me another apartment. I don't want to be in these chambers." The gun touched the man's shoulder. His golden brown eyes held steadfast to her eyes. "What's your name?"

"Bogdan." He didn't flinch, but instead pushed into the point of the gun with his shoulder. "I am here for your wishes." His voice was clear and he didn't hesitate with his words.

"Okay Bogdan. Find that apartment quickly. I want to take a bath." She lowered the gun.

He quickly moved away from her, "Yes Kyre." He punched the elevator button on the wall.

She laughed, "Get dressed first, Bogdan."

Chapter 14

"Hello, Baby. I miss you so much." James spoke softly into his cell phone. "I can't wait to see you darling. When can I come to you? I love you."

"I love you, too darling. Why don't you head to New York as soon as you can? I have found us a lovely apartment and I can't wait to see you."

"I'll drive there tonight." He answered eagerly.

The thought of James being with her in New York made her happier than she thought it would. The new apartment was on the other side of the city and nothing about it even remotely reminded her of the moments that she had spent with George. She stared out the windows and made mental plans of where she would take James. She pulled off her niqab, shook her hair from side to side and sighed. Her hands went unconsciously to the knife strapped to one leg and the gun she now carried strapped to the other. Bogdan had given her several guns and had explained to her that her best defense was herself. He had confided in her many details about the New York operation—things she needed to know to keep it all running smoothly. His loyalty had given her momentary pause, until Bogdan began to tell her how George had been such a cruel boss. His men had little respect for a man who tortured and murdered his own people. Bogdan gave her the names of dealers and buyers and he gave her the addresses of all the whore houses which George had control over.

Her respect for Bogdan grew proportionately. She found herself thinking about him that morning. He was young and strong. His light golden brown eyes were watchful. She liked his taste in furniture—black leather. He was practical. No white carpets like George. Hardwood floors—washable and solid. She stared at the people walking in the streets below her. Unlike George, she didn't see them as ants to be devoured. She saw them as human assets. She had told Bogdan to recruit as many of them as he could for her underground 'army'. She had told him with her voice steady, "I want to be the Kyre of hundreds." He in turn had told her that the fis already had hundreds of *family members,* but he also told her that it was better to have a loyal family than a dispersed large unhappy family. A loyal family would keep the Bese, the oath, which was sacred. Those that kept the Bese would protect her with their lives. Bogdan had knelt at her feet and proclaimed that Bese to her. She in turn had made him a part of her Bajrak, her executive committee. From that moment on, Bogdan was glued to Inayah's hip. No one came or went without his permission. He slept in the room next to hers, if indeed he slept at all. He watched over her drug trade, her arms deals, the trafficking of human organs.

Secretly, Bogdan wished to lift her khimar. He had never seen the face of his Kyre and obsessed about removing it, even in his sleep. Her musical voice, in her soft moments, seemed to reach his soul and then other times when she ordered the death of a coward and traitor, her voice sent chills up his spine. He felt that Inayah had earned her position. In all his years with George, no one had been able to eradicate the monster, only Inayah had gotten close enough to do so. Bogdan had tried to present women to entice George, but the man had only used them and then he killed them.

Bogdan's hate for George ran deep. The man had killed his mother and father and his older brother when he himself was just a boy. After their murders, Bogdan had no one to turn to and had been running barefoot in the streets when George offered him help. George had told him that his parents and brother were traitors to the cause and the monster then gave him food and a roof, but Bogdan never forgot the massacre that he had witnessed in his own family's home. He could still visualize them lying in their own black pools of blood in the middle of their kitchen floor. His mother's eyes kept staring at him from behind her niqab, as it turned a darker brown with the flow of her blood. Her eyes never blinked again, just stared at him, begging him to help her from the grip of their cold eternity. He had vowed that he would kill the man who had killed her, but he never had a clear chance to do so. The issue was that it seemed that George could predict his adversaries every move. The fiend kept him too close. Inayah was the only one who had infiltrated, not only George's chambers, but also his nefarious heart. Bogdan didn't understand this sovereignty she held over men's hearts, but he felt the tug on his own heart. He watched her eyes, shining and observant in their non-stop surveillance from her niqab. He imagined how her lips would appear, soft, supple and full. He obsessed about touching her long black hair that he knew was hidden under that niqab. Yet, he honored her; he respected her, but he also yearned to be with her night and day.

Inayah sensed his tension. She felt his desires and she manipulated his emotions to her advantage. Bogdan was not unlike most men, she could control him through this weakness that was much too transparent. Yet, seeing his weakness helped her expose her own flaws and failings with James. She silently agonized that James was her Achilles' heel. She vowed to herself that she would put a lock on her own heart. She began to unravel her feelings for James.

At first, when he arrived in New York, she would let him escort her to plays and dinners and she was seen often seen in public with her white gloved hand on his arm, but as her fears mounted, she would leave him home or not go out at all. She felt a storm brewing and she began to see, even him, as one of the dark clouds in her future. When they made love she became more and more demanding. She never let him believe that she was satisfied, so he walked around her with a sense of failure at not being enough for her. He watched Bogdan moving through her life, like the oil of a lava lamp, he slipped gently through her day. James became increasingly jealous of this 'other man' in her life.

"Inayah, I want you to dismiss Bogdan or move him to another place." James demanded.

She cocked her head left and right, like a bird of prey trying to figure out if an animal was too big to consume before sweeping down to destroy it. "He is my body guard." She answered simply.

"But I am man enough to protect you." He taunted with determination.

"No doubt," she smiled. "But aren't two heads better than one?"

James was silent.

"I have a meeting tonight." She began to put on her niqab. "I shouldn't be too late."

"Let me go with you." He pleaded.

"You know it is just a bunch of Muslims praying." She laughed and put her hands on his chest. "You would be bored to tears. No, just wait here for me."

"But lately you have meeting every night."

She kissed his mouth tenderly. "Do I? Oh my sweet, I don't think so. You are exaggerating."

His voice became agitated and impatient, "Am I? Well, let me tell you, you had one last night and the night before that. I want to know what is going on."

She kissed him again. "Nothing my love. We are clannish, you know that. We like to gather with each other and pray and..." She stopped.

"Women don't even pray with men." His voice was low and fell one step short of an all- out accusation.

She dropped her hands to her side. "We pray in separate quarters, but we do pray at the same time. Why do you think I carry this compass?" She reached into a hidden pocket and retrieved a small compass.

He nodded, "To face Mecca."

"Exactly. Unless you are entertaining thoughts of becoming a Muslim, I suggest you wait for me here." She put the compass back into her pocket. She kept her eyes steadily on his.

"I just want to be with you." His voice reflected his hurt.

"And I want to be with you, darling, but like I said, unless you are eager to convert, which of course, I wouldn't mind." She smiled, but when she saw the frown on his face, she added, "I thought not. I will see you soon, my love. I will not be long."

She left him there in the apartment, but he could hear the ruckus in the basement. The chanting rose up through the heater vents, punctuated with "Allah Akbar". The chant became so loud that he was determined to go downstairs and investigate. Once he arrived in the basement two guards blocked his path. One of the men was wearing a Moz, the traditional Holy War j'ihadist turban. The other man was wearing a Keffiyeh tied with a ekal, a black cord.

"Where are you going?" The one with the white Moz, stopped him from opening the door to the room where the meeting was being held. "You can't go in there."

"I can and will. Inayah is in there, correct?"

The man's hand went to his jacket pocket, "The Kyre is busy now."

James laughed, "Is she? Well, can you just tell her that her beloved James is waiting outside the door?"

The man shook his head. "Impossible. Please go back upstairs. The Kyre will be with you soon."

James raised his voice, "I want to see her now!"

The man with the Moz grabbed his elbow, "Let me see you to the elevator. Just go back to the room and she will be there soon. I will tell her you were here."

"Take your hands off me!" James pulled his arm away from the man's grip. "Who in the heck do you think you are? I demand you go get her right this moment!"

The man gave him a shove into the elevator. He growled, "I think you best leave now before something happens to you."

James locked his eyes with the man in the Moz, "Are you threatening me?"

"If you see it as a threat, then it must be so." The man answered softly. "Please go upstairs, at least to the lobby."

James entered the elevator and hit the key for the lobby. As he exited the elevator two men approached him. They were wearing black western suits. "Come with us." One of them grabbed his arms and lead him out into the street. "Where are we going? What you are you doing?" He began to struggle against the strong hold on his arm.

"Sir, we mean no harm. Just come with us peacefully and no one gets hurt."

James stopped struggling and allowed the man to guide him down the street and into a waiting car.

The man pushed him into the backseat, then slid in beside him. "Don't worry sir, we mean you no harm. I am Agent Wallace and the driver is Agent McKinley. We are with the FBI. We just want a few moments of your time."

Chapter 15

He didn't mean to, but he cried like a baby. The pain was just too much. The two agents stood silently by and let him continue to bawl, handing him tissues in moments of pause. "I don't know what's wrong with me. I knew something was wrong, I just kept looking the other way."

The two men nodded.

"She's beautiful you know, inside and outside."

They nodded again silently.

"I mean I can hardly believe what you are telling me." He shook his head, "I don't want to believe it."

The taller of the two men stepped forward with another tissue and handed it to James. "Believe it. It's all true. We have reason to believe that this Albanian cell is going to attack the president of the United States. We need your eyes and ears. Perhaps you heard her talking on the phone."

James shook his head. "No one talks in front of me. She has this guy who is her right arm, uh..."

"Bogdan."

"Yes, that's it, that's his name. He rarely leaves her side and when I'm there they don't talk about things. Usually they make me leave the room."

The shorter agent grunted. "Maybe you should refuse to leave the room."

James blinked and crushed the tissue in his hand. "Yeah, maybe so." He stopped crying. "I just can't imagine Inayah would be involved in such a thing, I mean a terrorist plot to kill the president. It's surreal. She is so sweet and kind and..."He stopped as he thought of how she had recently been abrupt in their love making. She had insisted that he wear the leather vest and boots she gave him and asked him to be submissive to the lash of a whip she brought into their bedroom. He thought she was just bored and wanted variety, after all, he had read *Fifty Shades of Grey*, but now, perhaps she really did intend to dominate him permanently! Maybe it wasn't a game for her to reduce her boredom.   "She has been less attentive lately." He admitted. He thought, *she pulls away from me and doesn't want to linger after love making, no matter what I do.* But he didn't confide in the two men about Inayah and his love making. He looked nervously at his hands in his lap. He hadn't really thought about any of it before, or maybe he had, but he dismissed it quickly, not wanting to think about the truth. He gingerly tip-toed through his mind, remembering her glances at Bogdan and how the man had smiled at her. *Was she having an affair right under my nose?* "What do you want from me?" He asked the two men.

"We ask that you just watch and listen. If you see or hear anything, call this number." He handed James a card. "We need to stop this."

James nodded. "Of course, I will help in any way I can. I'm sure it isn't her. I know she isn't involved , it has to be this Bogdan fellow. Since he came on the scene she has been a different woman."

The two FBI agents stood very still. They did not nod their heads, but stared into James' eyes. James continued awkwardly, "I mean, I haven't seen her do anything out of the ordinary." He waited for them to agree with him, but they did not.

"Just call if you find out anything." The taller one helped James up off the chair. "It will be greatly appreciated. Shall we drop you back at your apartment?"

James shook his head, "No, I think I will just walk around and clear my head a bit."

The two men nodded. The taller one opened the door, "We'll be in touch, James."

When he heard the door close behind him, he felt as if someone had poured ice water over his head. *Inayah a terrorist.* He bit his tongue with his front teeth, holding on tightly until he felt pain. *Inayah can't be a terrorist.* Then, he remembered her smile as the whip hit his legs during their sexual *play*. The reality nudged into his psyche, demanding recognition. Inayah relished giving him pain. The fact was that he knew she would be in unmeasurable joy right now if she could gaze into his grieving heart. He kept walking down the street, gulping at the air as if he were a fish laid on a countertop to die. He whispered, "None of this makes sense." He kept walking aimlessly, until the street lights came on. He slipped into a bar and took a seat at the end of the bar. "Bourbon, no water." He belched. "Keep 'em coming." The bar tender nodded and placed the full shot glass in front of him and in moments, poured him another.

In the lair of the apartment basement Inayah shouted at Bogdan, "Find him! Do you hear me? Why didn't you allow him to come in? We could have controlled him." She blurted, "He loves me." As soon as she said it, she regretted it. Bogdan's face shadowed as he frowned.

"And you? Do you love him, too, Inayah?" Bogdan reached out and touched her arm. She didn't recoil. He studied her eyes. "Well, do you?" His fingers closed on her arm with gentle pressure.

She breathed, "No."

Her "no" was the only word he needed to hear, he snatched her into his arms and pressed his body against hers, wanting desperately to raise her niqab, but stopping himself. "That's good." He murmured into her ear through the layer of material. His eyes stared unblinking at the drainage pipes crisscrossing the ceiling above their heads.

"He's a loose end." She said without emotion. "Bring him to me."

Bogdan's arms released her. "Of course." He didn't speak again, but left her standing there awash in her own tormented thoughts.

Do I really want James dead? Have I stopped loving him? She looked around the empty basement where unoccupied chairs were scattered—chairs where only minutes before had been full of men proclaiming their allegiance to her cause. *But IS it MY cause?* She asked herself. She closed her eyes as she tried to define *the cause*. Her mind reached out straining to pinpoint that cause, snatching at gossamer threads of childhood memories, of moments on her father's knee, memories of being with her mother, praying, and with her aunt Mahiba, scrambled with memories of her time with George and James. She saw snips of each moment, like a glued collage in her mind's eye. Sweat beads formed on her brow. Her legs were weak with the rubber of uncertainty. She put her hand to her head, as she tumbled into a nearby chair. The stark reality was there, right in front of her, clear-cut and undeniable. *I am going to kill James.* As soon as the thought materialized she shuddered with the chill that ran up and down her spine.

Chapter 16

James debated with himself if he should return to the apartment. He knew he was drunk. The bartender had helped him stand and sent him on his way into the dark street at two a.m. Very few people rambled in the streets and those that did were not faring much better than he. He decided in the fog of his drunken stupor that he would find a hotel and sleep off his stupefied depression. He glanced up and the down the street for the familiar sign of any hotel. A flashing neon red sign caught his eye with the words HO EL. Dazed he entered the lobby and muddled through the check in process.

When his head hit the yellowed pillowcase, there were no staggering thoughts still crossing his mind. The unyielding bed springs were ignored. Sweet oblivion drenched his entire body, however, morning's stark authenticity was accompanied by nausea and a clear-headed reality. As if to prove the existence of the horrid truth and its actuality, he said aloud, "Inayah is a terrorist." No amount of liquor had anesthetized or deadened that blatant reality. He glanced into the mirror and saw his bloodshot eyes ringed by purple dark circles. He leaned toward the mirror and repeated what he had said, "Inayah is a terrorist." The words stuck to his tongue like a fly on a strip of flypaper. He was so consumed by his own tortured thoughts, that he didn't recognize the insistent knock on the door until it had escalated to banging.

"Are you in there, James?"

He stood very still. He held his breath. He glanced around the room, searching for a weapon of defense and came up empty handed. The incessant knocking began again.

"James, I know you're in there." A toe of a boot kicked at the door. "Open this door."

James tried to place the voice. Had he heard it before? If so, where had he heard the deep male tones?

In the apartment, far from the impending intrusion into James' hotel room, Inayah paced impatiently in front of her latest visitor. He was dressed in a business suit. His hair neatly combed, his beard tightly managed around his masculine jaw. He held a black briefcase in his hand. Inayah stopped pacing and turned toward him, "How many do we need?"

The man shrugged his shoulders. "Ten. Fifteen perhaps."

Her dark eyes flashed behind her niqab. "I expect precision. How many?"

"Okay, to be safe, fifteen."

She smiled behind her veil. She enjoyed her moments of extreme power. Here in front of her was a powerful man, a man who consulted with the president of the United States, and yet, even he would do her every whim. She took a deep breath. All in the name of the *cause*. Her head began to spin, but this time, rather than spinning with images of indecision, her mind swooshed with images of carnage and destruction. "Procure them." She voiced clearly. "Fifteen." She locked her eyes on his, "All to deploy at once, of course."

The man nodded, "Of course."

She wondered how much she should trust this man. After he left the apartment, she summoned one of her own men to tail him with orders to execute him as soon as the deployment was accomplished. She had acquired the precise technique of her father...no loose ends. This man was definitely *a loose end. What was his motive?* She wondered. Then, she examined her own conscience, why wasn't it enough for her to hear the words *the cause* and know internally that it was the end- all answer? She poured herself a glass of ice cold water. She knew that the answer was simple. Each person has their own personal *cause;* their own personal reason for the things that they do in life. She stared out the apartment windows. Her thoughts competed with each other in her mind. As she looked out at the buildings of New York she began to feel as if someone was choking her; her throat constricted and she began to gasp for air. The reality was that she knew she needed to get away from this city or she would die here, but where would she go? She would wait here, until after the plans were accomplished and all was finished, then she would go. The *where* didn't matter right now. She just had to wait until it was done. As soon as she had the thought she said aloud, "But will it ever be done?"

Deep in the precincts of the barrio, in the hotel with no name, James was having his own reality. He knew that he could not run from whomever was banging on the hotel room's door. Whoever was banging on the door was determined to enter. He opened the door slowly. "Who are you?" he asked.

"FBI." The man shoved the door open.

"But you're not the guy I met before." James stepped back into the middle of the room. He could smell the stale alcohol on his own breath. His mind had cleared. He mentally made note of the bulge under the coat of the intruder.

"You're in danger." The man went to the window and pulled back the curtain to glance outside. "We have to go."

James stood with his feet wide apart, his eyes narrowed. "Why should I go with you? I don't even know who you are?"

The man jerked his head as he looked around the room, "I don't see any other of your friends in here. The way I see it, James, you don't have a choice, but to come with me."

James laughed, "Let's just say I would like to take my own life in my own hands. At least I have a pretty good idea of who I am."

The man shook his head, "You won't make it one city block. There's a hit out on you."

James began to roll down the sleeves of his crumpled shirt. He briefly asked himself, *when did I roll these up?* As he kept his eyes steadily on the intruder. "How do I know that you aren't the hit man?" He smiled nervously. His eyes continued to scan the room for anything that he could utilize as a weapon.

"James, for Pete's sake. If I was here to kill you, I could have done it already. Why would I even hesitate?" he shook his head, "Let's go. We are wasting time and we are sitting ducks if we stay here."

"You go on without me, Mr. uh, what did you say your name is?" James started for the door, if he hurried he could slam it behind him and make it to the fire escape at the end of the hall before the man could walk back across the room. Mentally, he timed his escape perfectly as he bolted for the door. He heard his feet hammering the bare linoleum as he headed for the fire escape. He climbed out on it and felt it clunk down with his weight. His foot stepped on the rungs and he mechanically moved one foot after the other. The street was four stories below him. He didn't even remember going up an elevator the night before. He glanced at the neon sign, now turned off and he could plainly see the word: Hotel with the "t". He didn't slow to look above him to see if he was followed. As soon as his feet hit the sidewalk he turned and ran. The only obstacles he encountered were early morning walkers. His shoulder bumped into them as he ran, but he didn't offer any apologies. He just kept running.

Inayah paced back and forth in front of Bogdan. "What do you mean he is gone? Gone where?"

"Our man was there, but he escaped. He's vanished." Bogdan unconsciously took a step back, away from the reach of Inayah's arms.

"What do you mean vanished? Do you mean like dead? That kind of vanished? You better mean that kind of vanish." She remembered her father explaining to her as a child that when people died they merely vanished, but were not really gone. One could lock them into memories and revive those memories as needed through-out one's life.

Bogdan coughed nervously. "He just disappeared. New York is a big city."

Inayah's eyes flashed, "Find him!"

Bogdan shook his head, "We are trying, Inayah. We will find him, it is only a matter of time."

"Trying? Trying is not doing! " She snatched a book off the coffee table and held it out to him, "Here, try to drop this book!" Her voice was shrill, "You either drop it or you hold it, there is not trying in this world!"

He stepped back another step.   Inayah's reputation proceeded her. Any moment he could feel her wrath slicing through his skin, as sharp and precise as her tongue. "Inayah, please, he is nothing to worry about. We will find him and eradicate him. We have other things, more important things to think about."

She dropped the book back on the table so hard that he thought that the glass tabletop might break with the force, but it did not. She reached for the knife on her leg and squeezed it, but did not pull the knife out. Bogdan was right, after all, James was a mere pawn and could in no way disrupt their plans. He was the gnat at a family picnic, swatted away with one slap of a hand. She nodded, "Yes, much more important things. Did the shipment arrive?"

"Yes, it's being distributed for sale even as we speak." His body relaxed when he realized that the conversation had moved on to a safer topic.

"Good. I have put the plan into motion. Soon the president of the United States will be dust." Even as she said it, she felt an uncomfortable constriction in her throat. There were so many "ifs" that came into play—'if he was there as planned, if the drones performed as programed, if there were no traitors in the quagmire of necessary agents, if some of the drones could get through the radar...' The 'if' list was endless, but she didn't allow herself any more moments of negativity. "We will succeed." She announced with certainty. She became aware of Bogdan's attempt to move away from her. She smiled inwardly at his fears. "Do you think I would kill you, Bogdan?"

He didn't answer.

"Well, do you?"

He took another step backwards. "Only a fool would underestimate your abilities." He answered, "And I am no fool."

"That is debatable." She laughed. "I would have to say that anyone who allows someone like James to escape has some properties of being a fool." She glared at him.

Bogdan swallowed hard. He should have realized that she had given him only a momentary reprieve. Inayah was relentless in her pursuit of perfection.

She continued, "James knows too much and now he is loose on the streets of New York with that knowledge." Her hand squeezed the knife on her leg tightly. "We all know one thing, knowledge is power." The words were spoken deep in her throat, in a guttural slur. "You have given him immeasurable power, Bogdan."

"I will find him."

"Yes, yes you will." She affirmed. "Leave me now. Find him. Those are your orders. Forget everything else I have commanded you to do. Find James and bring him to me. Is that clear?"

Bogdan nodded.

"Today." She added. "By nightfall."

He nodded silently again.

She moved towards him. His body stiffened as she put out her hands and pressed them against his chest. Her dark eyes caressed his face from behind her niqab. "I know I can trust you, Bogdan." Her voice was soft, mesmerizingly seductive. She leaned toward his face and he could feel her lips through the veil brushing against his lips, the thin layer of material stubbornly separating them. His desire was overpowering, he wanted to crush her lips with his, but he held back, as she barely pressed his lips with hers, speaking softly, directly into his mouth, "We will consummate our love soon," she whispered into his mouth, like the tongue of a snake, slithering in and out. He felt his body involuntarily press against hers, but just as soon as his body touched hers, she withdrew. "Now go! Finish what you have left undone." She turned and went towards the doors of her bedroom. She put her hand on the knob and then twisted her head to look back at him, "Bogdan, do not fail me again."

She disappeared behind the door. He heard the distinct click of the lock.

Chapter 17

James fumbled with the card in his fingers. Contacting the FBI was his only chance of evading the long reach of the Vezdek, the family. "Hello?" His voice was uncertain.

"James?"

"Yes, it's me. I need help. They're after me." His voice surged with new vitality.

"Don't worry, we can help you. Where are you?"

"I'm at the train station, next to the coffee vendor." James' eyes scanned the area around him.

"Don't move. I will be there within five minutes. You got it? Don't move."

"Yeah. Okay. I'll wait here." Before James pushed the button he added, "Hurry."

James leaned up against the brick wall. He watched as the coffee vendor handed cups of hot coffee to each customer before they rushed onto their trains. Women in pant suits, men in Burberry trench coats, women in stylish dresses, men in jeans...each person grabbed at their coffee with urgency. James entertained the thought of buying a cup for himself. His stomach growled, reminding him that he hadn't eaten anything since yesterday. He sauntered up to the vendor, "Coffee, cream, no sugar and one of those cinnamon rolls." Mimicking all the customers before him, he snatched at his coffee and the roll, but he did not get on a train, he walked slowly back to his place by the wall, like a crab returning to its place under a rock, only the wall didn't give him any protection. He was exposed, like a soft shelled crab waiting to be devoured by a seagull. It was as if he was lined up against the bricks, ready for a firing squad. He realized his situation, just in time. He slipped into a small stall, just in time to see two men, dressed in black trench coats, approach the coffee vendor. Neither of the men purchased a coffee. Their eyes darted across the train platform. They spoke briefly to the vendor and then their eyes jumped to the brick wall, crawled along it, until they landed on the entrance to the small stall where he had slipped in to find his brief asylum.

He saw them approach, like a black blur and felt the unmistakable vice grip on his arm. "James." He couldn't help but think of Shakespeare's line about a rose of any other name still being a rose. There was no way that he could hide. He let the vice grip lead him out onto the platform and then onto a train. The grip on his arm did not release until he sat on the bench on the train and the two men slid into the seat on either side of him. They rode in silence.

His thoughts pranced on the roof of his brain, They're FBI, I shouldn't be so afraid. I will just tell them what I know and that will be that. They'll find a safe place for me to hide until this is over, until she is captured. Even as he thought about her capture, he couldn't believe it. There was no reconciling with the reality. Inayah was a terrorist. He tried to absorb it, to make sense of it, but every time he thought of her soft voice, her gentle touch, the smoothness of her skin, nothing would compute. How can the woman I love be a terrorist? Then, he began to even examine his love for her. Do I love her? How can I love her? The tormenting thoughts continued to tsunami against him.

The men each grabbed his arms and lead him off the train. Within moments he realized that they were in front of Inayah's apartment. Before he could panic, they rushed him through the front doors to the elevator. He started to protest, but then, allowed them to push him into the elevator. Unexpectedly, the elevator didn't go up to her apartment, but down, to the basement.

He couldn't ignore the single chair placed under the blaring light bulb dangling from a pipe in the ceiling, on the plastic sheeting in the middle of the room . Nor could he ignore the brute force that plunged him into that chair or the tethering of his hands behind his back. He stared at the television suspended on a steel shelf. It was on, but the sound was turned off. He saw the stacks of other chairs in the corner of the room. The two men did not speak to him, but folded their arms and their eyes stared straight ahead as they waited. "What's going on? You aren't FBI, are you?" James voice shook, in spite of his efforts to control himself. Neither man looked at him. "Where is Inayah? I'm sure she wouldn't want me tied up in her basement!" The men did not even glance in his direction. He heard the elevator door open. Bogdan exited.

"So here you are, James. Finally." Bogdan grinned broadly. "Quite the illusive butterfly."

"Why am I here? Where is Inayah?" James' feet pushed against the floor in his attempt to free himself from the chair. He managed to wrinkle the plastic under the chair.

"James, James, James." Bogdan came closer to him with each pronunciation of James' name. Bogdan's accent irritated James.

"So James, tell me what you know."

"What? I don't know anything."

Bogdan shook his head. "You are Inayah's lover, isn't that correct?"

"That's none of your business!" James' feet continued to push at the floor. He managed to raise the back of the chair and then it fell back down again.

Bogdan took a knife from his waistband. "Many things ARE my business, James. For example, do you know that we are in the body parts trade?" He laughed when he saw James' surprised look. "Oh, so you didn't know. Well, we are. In fact, right now, as we speak, I have an order for a liver, kidneys, and a heart and guess what? I just happen to know where there are some nice fresh ones ready for delivery." His laughter echoed off the basement walls.

"You're mad! Release me immediately! Inayah is going to have your head for this."

Bogdan became instantly somber. "So you know how capable Inayah is. She will be here shortly." He paused and walked around James. "If it weren't for her, you would be dead already. I don't like to keep my customers waiting."

"She's going to kill you. You know that, right?" James threatened.

Bogdan put his head next to James' ear, "Perhaps," he hissed, "But not before she kills you."

"You fool! Inayah loves me! She will not tolerate this!" He screamed and squirmed, trying to loose his bindings. No sooner had it said it, when the elevator doors opened and Inayah appeared. She was completely covered in her Arabic dress. He tried to focus on her eyes.

"Inayah! Tell this man to release me! I told him you would not tolerate this." He banged his feet on the plastic.

She walked past Bogdan and stood in front of James. "Hello, James." Her voice was soft and melted in his ears. "This is so unfortunate." She whispered.

"Why are you doing this, Inayah? I thought you loved me."

She nodded, "I do. That's what makes it all so much more difficult." Her head jerked up towards the television. "Oh look, the White House is under attack." The entire White House was suffused in reddish orange flames. She quickly moved towards the TV and turned the knob for the sound.

A shocked announcer's voice reverberated, "Twelve drones were destroyed, but unfortunately three other drones made lethal contact. The president is now confirmed dead." She turned the knob again, turning off the sound. "So, it is finished." She looked at James. "Allah Akbar!"

His eyes widened with his terror.

When she saw the terror in his eyes, she walked up to the chair. "Don't be frightened, James. Love conquers all. I just had to make sure that you did not foil the plot, but now it is done. The viper is dead."

James slowly shook his head, "Don't you know that killing the president doesn't change a thing. The vice-president will take office and his views mirror the president's. Nothing changes. You could kill all of them and someone else will take their place. Your act is senseless and meaningless and..."

She turned toward Bogdan, "Leave us."

"But Inayah, you shouldn't be alone with him." Bogdan's hand reached out, but she moved outside his reach. "At least keep one of the guards here."

"All of you go." She waved her arm toward the elevator.

"I don't think this is wise, Inayah. Be reasonable." Bogdan pleaded.

She spoke slowly and deliberately, "Leave me." There was no mistaking her murderous tone. Bogdan and the two men moved toward the elevator. Once the doors closed, she faced James. Her voice was soft, alluring. "I didn't mean for you to become involved." Her hand went to her head and she removed her niqab. "This plan had been in place for some time for reasons that I won't explain now. It must suffice to say that your government officials wanted this, they paid highly for this." She knelt at his feet and rested her head on his lap.

He hated himself for wanting to caress her hair that fell like a black waterfall down his pant leg with his hand. When she looked up at him, her dark eyes were filled with tears. "There are things you would never understand. If you look inside a spider's web, the weave is often so complex that there is no unraveling it."

"Untie me." He beseeched her.

She shook her head. "Oh if only it were that simple." She lifted herself up, pushing on his knees and then she leaned into his mouth with hers, kissing him long and deep, reviving memories of their love-making, rekindling his desire for her, his deep love for her. She murmured, "I do love you, James, with what is left of my heart."

"Oh my sweet Inayah," he breathed. His jaded eyes didn't see the flash of the knife which plunged into his unsuspecting gut and then, that razor-sharp knife ripped up his body towards his throat, slicing cleanly between his rib cage, as if it were de-boning a chicken, and opening his throat. An unleashed river of blood spewed. He had no time for reverie.

She stood up and as she did so she wiped the knife on his pant leg, first one side of it and then the other, before lifting her skirt and sliding it comfortably back against her thigh. Her hand groped for her gun. She pivoted towards the elevator. She reached in her pocket and hit a button that immediately summoned Bogdan.

The steel elevator doors opened, not unlike the miniature doors of a small box-like stage. Bogdan and the two men stood facing her. She shot quickly, hitting Bogdan in the head first and then the other two. Bogdan fell across the path of the elevator doors. The doors repeatedly banged against his body as a bell sounded. She pulled his body into the basement room, entered the elevator with the other two bodies, and tapped on the lobby button. She readied her gun for the other three guards in the lobby. They fell in a barrage of bullets. She quickly went behind the counter where she had hidden a bag with her clothing. She stripped off her niqab and shinnied into the jeans and sweatshirt top. She shook her long black hair and then rolled all of it atop her head.

Without another thought, she stepped over a guard's body and headed for the front door. She ran her hand down her pant leg, wishing she had chosen a pair of much looser pants. She shoved the gun into her bra.

"Taxi!" She shouted as she stepped off the curb. The yellow cab swerved into the space. She yanked at the handle, "La Guardia." She smiled and blinked her eyes at the cab driver. Her head snapped back as he took off.

"Helluva thing the president being killed." The cab driver looked at her from the rearview mirror.

"Horrible." She responded.

"Can you imagine using those gosh damn drones to bomb the White House?" He continued to rattle on and then, honked his horn at a man crossing the street, "Outa the way asshole!" He then glanced at her again. "Those damn Arabs, what the hell are we going to do with them?"

She didn't answer, but blinked her dark eyes at him in submissive female confusion.

Chapter 18

She handed him the fare through the open window, making sure that her own fingers didn't touch the treated paper of the bill she slid in between the others. "Keep the change." She smiled at him. He winked, "Thanks lady!" Minutes later he would pull over to the side of the road as his head became dizzy and he felt his stomach beginning to cramp. The hospital would declare him dead due to a heart attack. She walked away from the cab content that he was not a loose end.

Her steps quickened now that she was in the airport. She headed to the lockers along one side. She pulled a key out of her pocket. She had memorized the number, locker 495. She slid the key into the lock and the locker popped open. She grabbed at the small beige suitcase. She placed the suitcase on the floor, opened it quickly to retrieve an envelope. She smiled when she saw the pretty blue dress and matching blue purse she had bought for her plane ride to Turkey. She snapped the suitcase closed. She put the envelope in her pocket. She carried the suitcase to the lady's room, so that she could change her clothes.

When she emerged from the bathroom she was wearing the light blue silk dress, two inch black heels, and carrying the blue matching handbag over her shoulder with the envelope safely tucked inside it. She had double-checked her paper work, all was in order. She wrapped the locker key in tissue and tossed it into the trash container. She stuffed her jeans and sweatshirt into the suitcase. Now, it was only a matter of boarding the plane with her knife and gun.

She got in line to go through the check point. She complained to the lady in front of her that her stomach was hurting. The woman was sympathetic. "Maybe you ate something. I know there are a chain of restaurants having issue with their produce. Did you have a salad?"

"Yes, as a matter of fact, I did." She placed her hand on her stomach.

"Oh, I hope you didn't get some of that tainted food!" The woman reached out and touched Inayah's hand with her fire red nails.

Inayah had put a piece of yarn in her mouth and now began to gag, "Oh dear, I think I'm going to vomit." She announced.

The woman panicked, "Excuse me! This woman is going to puke! Do you have a bag or a bucket?"

The attendant on the x-ray machine hurried around the machine. "Are you alright mam?"

Inayah began to vomit. The security attendant grabbed her arm and rushed her through the check point. "Why don't you just sit here until you feel better? Here's a trash bucket for you in case you have to puke again."   She handed the metal trashcan to Inayah. Inayah nodded silently and began to vomit again as the yarn was still caught in her throat. A flight attendant from the air plane came to her side, "Let's get you boarded and comfy. Are you sure you don't want to cancel your trip until you feel better?"

"I have to go." She whispered.

"Okay then, let's get you on board."   The attendant took her elbow and guided her onto the plane. She gave her a can of Seven-Up and a glass of ice. She placed a blanket over Inayah's knees. She secured the beige suitcase in the overhead, as she watched Inayah gagging again. She handed her a blue plastic bag, "Here, in case you need to vomit again." She shook her head, "You must be miserable."

As soon as the attendant was gone, Inayah removed the yarn from her throat and tilted back her seat. Her eyes scanned the plane. All seemed to be in order, nothing seemed suspicious or out of the ordinary. She closed her eyes. This was going to be a smooth, uneventful ride.

Istanbul was exactly as she remembered. She hadn't been there since her trip with her father when she was a teenager. She inhaled deeply, taking in the scents of the city. The Four Seasons at the Bosphorus was as elegant as she remembered. She found her way to the bright orange cushions on the patio. From here she could watch the ships as they passed by, which would give her something to do while she waited. She didn't have to wait long before he appeared. He immediately leaned over her and kissed her forehead, "Darling, have you been waiting long?" She sniffed the scent of Dolce and Gabbana. "I've missed you terribly."

She looked into his blue eyes and felt her heart skip a beat. "I've missed you, too."

He slid into a chair beside her. "I thought we would never see each other again." She whispered.

He slipped his arm gently around her shoulders, "How could you even think such a thing? You knew I would be waiting at the end of the long dark tunnel." He kissed her cheek. "I am so sorry about your father." His finger outlined her mouth and then he kissed her lips.

"Yes, me too. He became collateral damage." She tried to keep her voice unemotional and detached.

A waiter came to their table, "Will you be dining on the patio this evening?"

"What do you think, sweetheart? Do you want to eat here or in our room?" His hand squeezed her shoulder.

"Perhaps in our room."

He nodded, "Of course." He helped her stand and then lead her past the expansive pool to the elevator. "I imagine you have jet lag," he spoke into her ear.

"Slightly. Oh, can we retrieve my suitcase at the reception?"

He released her shoulders, "Yes, of course darling. I should have been more alert to your needs." He asked the concierge to bring her suitcase up to their room.

The hotel room was absolutely stunning. Her eyes scanned the silver ice bucket, the plump pillows on the bed. "Would you like a glass of wine?" he asked in their awkward moment of silence. "I sense your tenseness. We have been apart too long." He began to pour a glass of white wine before she could answer. He handed it to her as she sat down on the edge of the white bedspread. "How long has it been?" He asked.

She sighed, "Years."

He nodded and sipped his wine. "Years." He looked out the window, "Istanbul. I would have preferred London or Paris." He kept looking out the window. "At least I know those cities, but Istanbul is so foreign to me."

"And I as well." She added. "But we cannot ignore our orders."

He turned to look at her, "Can't we?" She wondered if he was challenging her. She also wondered if she still loved him. "Eitan," she paused, "Do you still love me?" She dragged it out of herself.

He immediately wrapped her in his arms, "Of course my love! Nothing has changed. What is a small span of time? Nothing for two hearts so locked together as ours." He kissed her lips and held onto her. "Nothing can come between us, not time, not oceans, not people, not our duty..."he paused, "You are my wife."

She closed her eyes tightly. Would your wife sleep with other men? Would your wife murder others? Would your wife look at you with suspicion? She nodded, "Yes, I am your wife."

Eitan Bachmann was definitely her husband. He was also an Israli officer in the MOSAD. Her father, himself, had blessed their union. Eitan was wrapped up in the *cause* as tightly as she was, maybe even more tightly. As inconceivable as it seemed, even implausible, the Jew and the Arab were united, not only in matrimony, but in the affairs of state. She whispered, "Can I speak?"

"The room has been cleared." He glanced into the corners of the room. "Speak freely."

"Am I finished now? Can it stop?" she asked.

He fell to his knees at her feet and kissed the palms of her hands. "I wish, my sweet, I wish it could stop. But no, it isn't finished. There is still much to do. There is no turning back now." He reached up and touched her cheek feeling her soft skin under his fingertips. "You know that the American president had to go. He was the enemy of Israel."

Tears filled her eyes, "But so many people I..." Her moment of personal pain shocked her. She tried to harden her heart, but she continued to feel waves of compassion rolling over her. "I killed so many people."

"A soldier must do these things. Don't look back, my angel." He kissed her cheek.

"I killed people who loved me." She looked into his eyes, "Doesn't that frighten and worry you?"

He shook his head, "Absolutely not. You didn't love these men. You had no attachment to these men. They were our enemy and you did what you had to do. I have done the same, but it has nothing to do with us, my darling. The kidon must do what it must do." He saw that her body was stiff, perhaps not from fear, but from her own disgust of herself and who she had become. Inayah had become a perfect killing machine, except unlike most of them, she was unable to lose her heart, therefore she eroded her own perfection. In many ways, he was much like her. She had captured his heart long ago and there were many times that he wished he could eradicate her from his thoughts, but her dark eyes were always there in the recesses of his brain, lurking, tantalizing him, making him lose his grip on the prison where he had locked his own heart. "You are much too hard on yourself Ina."   He had shortened her name to his endearment of her.

"Do you have the new orders?" She asked him boldly.

"Let's not talk of work, shall we? We haven't seen each other in years and already you are eager to talk of work. Frankly, Ina, I am disappointed in you." He wrapped a strand of her hair around his finger and tugged gently. "Don't you want to spend some time wrapped in my arms after such a long time?"

She nodded. When she had first met him at the Henzelia, the school for MOSAD operatives near Tel Aviv, she had been much younger, of course, and he was older and she found his presence captivating. He had taken her under his wing, gently coaching her and helping her become one of their best female agents. At Henzelia she learned that a female's body was her grand weapon and that having sex with the enemy gave a woman opportunities that a man could never have. Her father approved of him immediately when she told him all about Eitan, but her father had also cautioned that in their line of work there was no room for true love. She wondered if her father had ever loved her mother. She played back the memory of her mother's death and saw vividly her father's detachment as they left her body there in the car. Was that love? If you loved someone, do you just walk away when they die? I walked away from George, from James...she felt her eyes attempting to fill with tears. She fought the tears and rubbed at her eyes with the back of her hand. *Didn't I barely flinch when I knew my father had been killed?* Her eyes scanned Eitan's face. *Do I love Eitan?* She tormented herself with the question. She did not have the answer; she only knew that she loved to look into his bright blue eyes and breathe in his masculine scent, and nuzzle her face in his neck while his hands explored her body.

Their love making reignited her heart and she let his love wash over her and seep into her pores until she remembered, that yes, she did love Eitan. She lay in the crook of his arm, her black hair sprawled over his chest, as he clasped her hand in his. "I love you near me like this." He whispered in her ear. "We must never be apart so long again." Even as he said it, he immediately knew that he had no control over what happened in their lives. He and Ina were Katsas, field agents, and they could be ordered anywhere in the world at any time. Yet, right now, right this moment in time, he had her in his arms. He could protect her; he could make love to her; he could promise her his love and his devotion to the ends of time. What bothered him most was that she didn't believe him.

They fell asleep with the quiet hum of the room's fan in the background. He kept his arm around her and his face nuzzled against her hair. Both of them startled when they heard the ringing of the phone. Eitan answered. "Yeah." He listened intently and then silently hung up the phone. He turned to her, "Orders."

"For both of us?" She asked.

He nodded. There was no light in his eyes. "Yes, for both of us."

When he took her hands in his and told her their orders, she sat very still. Finally, she wriggled her hands away from his and stood. She walked over to the window and looked out at the lights across the water. "So we are to leave Istanbul?" She inhaled deeply. "I am once again to follow the training of Masluh and shake off any tail that the enemy might have put on me." She was reciting her lines, as if they had been fed to her. "I am to go to Los Angeles and connect with the Katsas there. I am to kill..." She stopped short of saying anyone's name. "How can we be sure that these people are there?"

Eitan shook his head, "The one thing we know from our experience, Ina, we cannot wait to move on the basis of certainty. Nothing is certain." He put his hand on her shoulder and turned her towards him. "Nothing."

"That IS certainty, Eitan. We can be sure that nothing is certain and in that there is certainty." She smiled and touched his cheek. "Word games in our last moments when we should just be making passionate love. Who knows when we will be together again, my sweet dear husband."

He pulled her to him and held her so tightly that she could barely catch her breath. "We will defy them, Ina, we will not do this mission. We will go to New Zealand and lose ourselves in the outback. Please, Ina, say you will do this with me."

"Oh Eitan, I want to, I really want to just run away with you and hide where no one will ever find us."

His words gushed out of his mouth, "We can, my love! All we have to do is plan it and we can make it happen. At least our training has given us that ability."

She shook her head, "No, my love, we don't have the ability to disappear that well. No one does; they will kill us." She laughed softly, "And then we won't be able to make love again for sure."

"This is nothing to joke about, Ina. I don't want to let you go. I want us to be together forever without MOSAD as our bed partner. I don't want to answer the calls in the middle of the night and then traipse off to some hell hole to murder someone I don't even know."

Inayah whispered, "I go, and it is done' the bell invites me."

"You think Shakespeare's words are going to provide us with comfort for having to say good bye again?" His voice rose in anger.

She put her finger to his lips to silence him. "If Shakespeare annoys you, then how about if I quote Cowper, are you equally angry with him?" She smiled. "Absence from whom we love is worse than death, and frustrates hope sever than despair."

He crushed her body against his. "We won't do it, Ina! I refuse to let you go off again. I am going to make a plan, a real plan to get us to New Zealand, away from everything, where we can be together." He kissed her passionately and then said, "I have people there who I can rely on."

She tossed her head back, "More Mossad?"

"No, not like that, real friends." He spoke quickly. "Let's plan to meet there, in New Zealand. I have this friend, Joe Everton, he has a ranch and..."

She interrupted him, "You are being ridiculous, we have no friends, nor will be ever have any friends and if we did we would have to kill them." She turned and walked to the bathroom, locking the door behind her. She placed her hands on the marble and leaned over the sink to look into the mirror. She thought, *This is the face of a terrorist.* She looked at her hands. *These are the hands of a terrorist.* She shook her head, "I don't look any different than anyone else." She continued to stare at herself. "Killing the ISIS leader will be an easy task. I just need an Abaya and a niqab." Her hand brushed against her leg where her knife was securely strapped. "And my friend here." She patted the knife affectionately, as if the knife was a breathing, living entity. She looked intently into the mirror and said aloud, "I lied." Her lips curled into a sinister smile. "I do have a friend."

When she came out of the bathroom, Eitan was gone. She knew that he would be. He had to go, just as she had to go. Duty made life simple. She looked around the room to see if he had left her a note. He had not. She knew he wouldn't, but something in her heart made her check for a note anyway. She spied the wad of money on the dresser. The money was better than a note. She began to get dressed and shoved the American bills into her jeans' pocket. She fumbled through her suitcase, as she looked for her American passport. When she found it, she opened it quickly: Ina Steinbrunner. She instantly decided that she liked that name. She removed the knife from her leg strap and sheared her hair around her face to match the picture of Ina Steinbrunner. The wisps of her hair framed her face in curved curls.

She allowed herself a brief moment to think of Eitan. "I will see you again." She vowed as she snapped the lid of her suitcase closed. But yet, thoughts of widowhood entered her mind, without her even knowing the horrific thoughts were there. "Eitan, I swear I will kill you if you dare die." She chuckled at her own attempt at humor.

Chapter 19

"Now Sally, remember not to drink the water here in Los Angeles. It's recycled from toilets." A woman grabbed her daughter's hand as they hurried through the airport. Her eyes shifted left and right and continued to do so as she hurried along. Inayah pulled her beige suitcase through the crowds, keeping the pace of the people around her, until she went out the automatic sliding doors into the street.

"Rental car agency?" She asked one of the tall Black men checking in travelers' luggage.

"There's a shuttle." He pointed to a bus parked in front of the exit doors.

"Thank you." She continued down the sidewalk towards the shuttle bus. She yanked her suitcase up the step into the bus.

The driver smiled, "Welcome aboard. Where to?"

"The rental car agency." She ordered.

"Which one, Avis, Hertz, National?" The woman driver adjusted her posture, sliding her large rear end from side to side impatiently.

"Avis, I guess." She pushed her suitcase onto the rack and then sat down. She thought about how interesting it would be to drive the Los Angeles freeways. Her rented townhome was in the small town of West Hills, about an hour away, if the freeway traffic wasn't too bad. She definitely would purchase a GPS to get around while she was here. She looked up and saw the little girl and her mother she had seen before entering the bus. The little girl was whining again about wanting a drink of water.

"Sally, I am not going to tell you again. We are not going to drink out of the fountains. It's pee pee water." The mother yanked on the little girl's hand and pulled her into the shuttle bus. Inayah continued to watch them. She wondered if she would ever have a child of her own and if she would, indeed, be a good mother. She watched as the mother focused on her cell phone while the little girl chatted, "Are we going to Disneyland today, mommy? I want to see Mickey Mouse, will he be there, mommy? Mommy can we see Snow White, too?" She continued to ask her mother questions which her mother never acknowledged, nor did she answer. The mother just continued to concentrate on the screen of her cellphone. Inayah wondered if she would end up ignoring her children that way. She stared out the bus window. I am not having children, so why am I even thinking about this? She did not look at the pathetic little girl again, perhaps she should have.

Driving to the townhome wasn't difficult once she got on highway 101. She exited at Topanga and drove past the upscale shopping centers. The new Village was all lit up with twinkling white lights. She thought briefly about buying a new dress, just in case Eitan found his way back to her. Something inside her told her that he would, but she realized that the idea was far-fetched. He had undoubtedly been sent to another part of the world. She was here for the special final days of Ramadan. Her objective was clear. There were many things she needed to buy and none of them included the purchase of a new dress. There would be explosives and of course she would have to have keys to get into "places". Killing the ISIS leader would not be an easy endeavor. He was layered with guards and protocol, but he was not immune to the whiles of a woman, that she had researched. He had a weakness for food and for women, he also enjoyed skiing. She couldn't ski, but he wouldn't know that, of course. The plan was already formed in her mind's eye. She looked at her watch. She would be at the townhouse before dark. There would be plenty of time to drive to the Home Depot or a Lowes to purchase the things she needed. Perhaps she would go to both, to keep suspicion at a minimum. She had taken the courses on how to make a bomb, how to poison someone without recognition of the agent used, and she was very knowledgeable in techniques of how she could remain stealth and get what she needed accomplished. She took a deep breath. *I wanted out and here I am, neck deep, ready to murder again.* The thought of the chase and the ultimate goal excited her and caused her adrenaline to begin to pump into her veins. She began to drive the rental car even faster, as if she was keeping up with the beat of her heart. She looked in the mirror and saw the red light flashing behind her. Carefully, she pulled the car over the five lanes to the side of the freeway.

She stared blankly at the officer. "You're kidding, right? I couldn't have been going more than 65."

"Admission of guilt," he said and smiled. "You're in a 55 zone. May I see your license and registration?"

She dug in her purse for Ina Steinbrunner's ID. Then she leaned over and opened the glove box and retrieved the rental car's registration. "I just got here from overseas. I think I have a bit of jet lag." She offered, hoping to get some sympathy, but the officer ignored her and continued to write the ticket.

When he was done, he scribbled across the top: Warning.

"Oh, thank you officer!"

"Just don't let it happen again." He winked at her and returned to his motorcycle.

She watched him climb onto it. "Now you've done it," she said aloud. "Now I have to kill you." She had pricked his skin with a very thin needle. He didn't even feel it. She gunned her car engine and sped away knowing that he would be dead within minutes. No one must know her face. She yearned to hide behind her niqab, but here in West Hills she would obviously not *fit in*. She desperately wanted to blend in—somewhere, anywhere. But she had so much to do. She turned into the gated community, gave the guard the particulars he needed and was grateful to be able to just park the rental car and go into her temporary home.

She flipped the switch of the entry chandelier. Light flooded the living room and entry. She spied a large recliner. She collapsed into the large soft brown chair on the left side of the entry door. Normally, she would have scanned every inch of the townhome, looking for listening devices, booby traps, or intruders, but she closed her eyes and let sleep wash over her jet-lagged body. The chair felt like giant arms hugging her and she snuggled into them, her face brightly lit from the overhead chandelier.

Upstairs, the floorboards creaked with the step of a heavy boot, but Inayah was oblivious to the sound, lost in her deep fathom of sleep. A hooded shadow passed by the mirror hung on the wall by the stairs and then the shadow became motionless, watching. A flash of sharp steel caught the light from the entry chandelier, reflecting the sliver of light in the stairwell darkness.

Within seconds the shadow was next to the over-stuffed easy chair. A heavy hand clasped tightly on Inayah's mouth, making her startle quickly to action, but it was too late. She was over-powered by the hooded shadow dressed all in black.

"I'm ashamed of you, Inayah. I have never seen you so careless."   She recognized the deep masculine voice immediately, as the hand let go over her mouth.

"Eitan!" Her arms clasped around his neck. "How did you get here?"

He shook his head, "I'm disappointed in you, my love." He reached into his pocket, "I found these hidden devices here and that was just my first sweep. No telling what else is here. The point being, someone else knows you're here."   He looked into her eyes, "I could easily have slit your throat."

Her eyes jumped around the room realizing that he was saying the truth. She hadn't taken a moment to check out a single thing, perhaps for the first time in her career. This omission could very well have been her last. She nodded silently, immediately regretting that they had spoken out loud. She put her finger to her mouth. She stood up and grabbed her bag which she had flung in the entry and tip toed towards the front door. He followed. They left the chandelier glowing. They got into his car.

He drove up the coast. Neither of them spoke. She was lost in the stark ice reality of how foolish she had been, how utterly careless. She watched out the window as restaurants, furniture stores, condos and apartments sped by. Eitan seemed to know exactly where he was going. He reached over and squeezed her hand, "Close your eyes sweetheart. It's a ways and you can rest safely." His smile assured her. She nodded and closed her eyes.

When she opened them again it was when the car stopped moving. Her first sensation was his hand still holding hers. She smiled at him, "Thank you. I needed that. I've never been so tired in my whole entire life."

"It's alright sweetheart. At least this time it was me who woke you up and not them."

"Yes, but they know I am here. Who told them?"

"They have their ways. But this is a safe house." She looked at the tiny beach shack. The porch was about to cave in and she was certain that the roof would leak if California got real rain. Once inside she marveled how Eitan knew where everything was housed, even the ship to shore radio.

"You have been here before?" He didn't answer, but continued to take electronics out of hidden boards and cupboards. "I have my orders," he stated bluntly. "And you have yours."

She watched him signing onto a computer. "We don't have the same order, do we?" she asked with some concern in her voice.

"Maybe, but we can't discuss it. Darling, why don't you do what you have to do and I will do what I have to do and then we can go get a bite to eat?" He was already deep into his tasks. She nodded. The one thing she knew about Eitan after all these years was that business always had to come first. His disappoint with her was genuine. He believed that she had failed herself and ultimately him, but he said no more about it.

She held her hand to her head. She felt dizzy and extremely tired. "I think I am getting sick, Eitan." He didn't look up. She no longer existed for him. He was deep into his work. She felt a lurch in her stomach and asked urgently, "Where is the restroom?" He never looked up to answer her. She went down a small hall and found the restroom on her own. It was a bathroom sandwiched between two bedrooms. She sat on the closed toilet lid and put her hand on her head. This was not a great time to get the flu! She heard the unmistakable mumbling of two voices punctuated with static coming from the room where she had just left Eitan. She strained to hear what the voices were saying. "Urgent. Couldn't be avoided. Yes. Will neutralize. Simplify. Yes. No second chance." The static stopped when the voices stopped. She stood and splashed some cold water on her face from the old crusted water spout.

The knock at the door made her jump. "Yes?"

"Inayah, I need to speak with you." He paused, "Are you okay?"

"I'm ill." She wiped the sweat from her brow. "I must have eaten something bad."

"Are you going to be alright, sweetheart?"

She waited a few seconds before she answered, "Yes, I'll be alright. Just need to rest a bit." She sat back down on the toilet lid. "I'll be out in a moment."

He didn't speak again.

Her head continued to spin. She stood up and vomited into the toilet. She instantly felt better. She washed her face and left the bathroom. "What is it darling?" She asked.

He clicked his fingers on the computer and then snapped the lid shut. "He's here."

"He who?" She asked.

"You know who, Inayah. You don't have to be secretive with me." His eyes twinkled as they looked at her, but she knew he was baiting her. Of course she had to be secretive. Both their lives depended on it.

"I don't know who you are talking of, sweetheart." She smiled. "Any food in this place?

I just up-chucked. I must have got a bug. I feel much better now."

He pointed to the other room, "A few things in the fridge and in the cupboards. Mainstays. Crackers, soup. Things that keep. I don't know how long I will be here, or you either for that matter."

She put her hand on his shoulder, "I never expected to see you here in California and certainly not with me. I mean it's like a miracle. They finally are letting us work together."

He shook his head, "We aren't working together, we are working parallel. One of us is the back up." He paused and turned to look at her again. "In case the other fails."

She felt her knife heavy on her thigh. She wanted to say, *We don't fail*. But then, she would have had to explain the 'we' and she didn't feel like doing so. She walked away and went into the small kitchen. She grabbed a bag of Saltine crackers and sat at a small table. She put the corner of one white cracker in between her teeth and just sat there, not biting it, just thinking. A thought was rising to her consciousness, *How did Eitan know where I was? Even if they had the same mission we wouldn't have been expected to stay in the same place. The overlap would be too dangerous.* She looked toward the living room. A heavy lump formed in her throat. *But he could have killed me and didn't. If he is a double agent, why wouldn't he? Or even if he isn't a double agent and had orders to kill me, he would have done it right then. Wouldn't he?* She bit down on the cracker and chewed thoughtfully. Her stomach lurched again. *Damn! Of all things to get a stomach flu now when I am supposed to be at my most commanding.* She watched Eitan coming towards her.

"Find something?" He asked nonchalantly.

She nodded silently, her mouth full of crackers.

"Good. I'm going out for a while. Make yourself comfortable."

She knew enough not to ask where he was going. He might not even come back and she would just have to accept it as the way it is. "Okay." She answered numbly. She felt the cracker sticking in her throat.

"Inayah," He put his hand on her arm, "I know this seems, well, it seems..." he paused. "I want you to know I love you dearly."

Her eyes rolled up to stare at him. "I love you, too Eitan."

She wanted to add that love had nothing to do with anything she was feeling at that moment, but she didn't. She wanted to ask him things she knew he couldn't answer. He undoubtedly had things he would want to ask her in turn, but he didn't ask. The palm of his hand went to her cheek, "Stay safe until I get back, Inayah."

She nodded, "You, too." Nothing felt right or normal to her. She went to the window to watch him go. She saw him get into a stranger's car. A woman was driving. Her heart sank as a chill ran through her body. She glanced around the small cottage and saw her beige suitcase. She grabbed at the handle and walked out the door. Something told her that the little cottage was not a refuge at all, but some kind of trap, perhaps Eitan didn't even know it, yet the thought lingered much too long in her head, perhaps he did...

Chapter 20

She walked down several busy streets and tried to hail a taxi, but found that the town of Camarillo definitely had a shortage of readily available taxis cruising the streets for eager riders. She finally called one of the cab companies and a cab was sent to her. Once in the cab she adjusted her backside on the cracked leather. "Do you know of a nice hotel?" She asked.

"Me? Lady, I just drive, I'm not a travel agent." He kept his eyes straight ahead. She could see his eyes in the mirror. Every now and again he stared at her.

"Okay, can you drive me to Santa Barbara?" she asked remembering that she had found several hotels there that would be suitable—and closer to her target.

"It'll cost you lady. That's almost an hour depending on traffic."

"Yes, I'm quite aware," she said. "I'll pay."

He shrugged. "Sure, Santa Barbara it is. Half fare up front." He put his hand over the backseat with his palm up for her to put the money in. Far away she heard a voice in her head, "Alms for the poor. Alms for the poor." She shook her head so that image vanished.

She watched the Pacific Ocean passing on the left of the cab's windows. The ocean was calm, like glass. She could see for miles. Seagulls swooped over the water and pelicans dove in. The picturesque scene was like a living painting. She pressed her forehead against the window. If only she could just stop the cab and walk along the white sand, feeling it squish between her toes. If only she could leave her knife and gun forever behind. Her stomach began to wretch. "Pull over a moment," she ordered. The cab swerved to the side. She yanked open the door and spewed vomit on the warm black asphalt.

"You okay lady?"

She slammed the door shut as she got back in. "I'm fine. I think I ate something on a plane that didn't agree with me."

"Uh, yeah, we have had so much trouble lately with restaurants with bad food. Maybe you got some of that. Mostly Mexican cuisine. Did you eat Mexican food?"

She wiped her mouth with a tissue. For the first time she had second thoughts. "No, just a salad or something." Now, she was feeling fine. If she was ill, she shouldn't she still be ill? Her mind began to assess her feelings. She had no headache. No stomach ache. Why was she still sick?

Like a huge water balloon hanging over her head, the thought popped, as if splashing cold water over her, the thought drenched her thoughts. *Am I pregnant?* She sat very still and placed both her hands on her stomach, as she counted back the days and her times with Eitan. She grabbed at her cell phone and pulled up a calendar. Air gushed out of her mouth in shock silent reality. *I am pregnant.* Se blinked her eyes at the stark authenticity. She kept her hands on her stomach and felt her entire body tingle. *I'm a mother.* No sooner did she have the thought then she removed her hands from her stomach and her hand brushed her leg and she felt the butt of her gun. *How can I be a mother? What would Eitan think of becoming a father?*

She brushed all her thoughts out of her mind. There was no room to think of Eitan or of a baby or anything else right now. She had one objective. Her eyes narrowed. She forced herself to control her own thoughts. So, there was a new mosque in Goleta and the target would be there visiting. She knew that much. Goleta was close to Santa Barbara, a mere ten minutes. She began to formulate her plan in her head. The Muslim center was on the corner of Los Carneros Road and Calle Real. The Islamic Society's leader had announced the arrival of the target on their Facebook page. The target would be giving a lecture, almost too easy for her. She wondered if Eitan had the exact same orders.

Simple, she thought, but then, her hand pressed against her stomach. The stakes were higher this time. She had to make it out of there. No martyrdom for her. She was the capsule holding a new life. She had to survive in order to protect her child, their child, hers and Eitan's child. She sighed heavily. This mission would be her most difficult ever. This time she cared if she lived or died. This was the first time in her life that she needed to stay alive.

The motel faced the harbor. The room afforded her a good view of all the bicyclists, skaters, and casual walkers or runners along the water's edge, but she did not look out the window. She was concentrating on a map she had rolled out on the table. She began to plan her every move for tomorrow. She took a pen and marked all the available exits. She highlighted the roads that when in and out of the area and began to memorize them. She would be driving a rental car and needed to know every possible way of escape. Night had fallen before she was finished. She clicked on the overhead light above the table. Her eyes moved over the map; satisfied that she had memorized it, she began to roll it up.

She spoke to the four walls, "I'm hungry. I think I need some good ol' comfort food carry out." She took a colorful book from the bedside table and began to glance at the pictures. She dialed room service. "I'd like to order a pizza." She smiled wondering if the baby wanted pizza. Probably not. She was going to have to take better care of herself from now on. No more assassinations. She knew tomorrow would go as planned, but she still had a gnawing feeling. This time she had someone else to worry about. She placed her gun on the table. "I will be extra cautious," she reminded herself out loud. Even the pizza man was suspect. She hid behind the door and offered him the money around the edge. He never saw her face. "Keep the change." She said as she slammed the door shut feeling very smug that she didn't have to kill him.

She opened her beige suitcase and took out her niqab. She would slide into the crowd, unnoticed, a viper among vipers. She quickly dressed and sat in the chair looking at the pizza box. She kept staring at it until she couldn't stand it anymore. *Am I that paranoid?* She asked herself. The answer was a definite, yes. She took the box, opened the door and threw the box as far as she could into the parking lot below. The pizza box exploded as soon as it hit the ground. She slipped out the door, leaving her empty suitcase behind. She heard the sirens blaring as she walked down the street, her niqab blowing in the ocean breeze.

When she heard, "Sister, hello." She turned to see a woman dressed in identical clothes. "Are you here for the lecture tomorrow?"

Inayah nodded as she summed up the woman who had come from behind. That alone made the hairs on her arms stand up. The woman had come from the hotel, just as she had.

"Something exploded in the hotel parking lot. I thought it best to just leave. You know how some people feel about Muslims." The woman was now within arm reach.

"Yes, I heard it. Were you staying in the hotel?" She asked.

The woman nodded, "I was, but now I don't know where to go. I certainly don't want to stay in a hotel that has things exploding in its parking lot."

Inayah smiled, "Maybe we can find another hotel."

"I doubt it. Do you know how important the lecturer is? There are so many Muslims here you would think it was Mecca." She smiled, but Inayah couldn't see her smile behind the niqab. The woman's eyes shone brighter and they crinkled in the corners, so it seemed she was smiling.

"Yes, I do know. Well, perhaps we shall have to just go there and camp out until tomorrow morning." Inayah started walking toward the new Muslim center.

"You mean, sleep outside?" The woman's eyes became even wider.

"I won't sleep. I will just wait there." Inayah kept walking. She figured there was safety in numbers. If the woman was a terrorist, she wouldn't want to kill so many Muslims at once just kill her. Was her cover blown? She kept walking and the woman kept up with her.

"My name is Tahira." The woman reached out and touched Inayah's sleeve.

"I am Widad. Are you here alone?" Inayah gave a fictitious name and asked the one question that was bothering her. How many more like Tahira were following her?

"I'm alone. I want to hear him lecture."

Inayah nodded, "Me too."

The night was cool and their clothes afforded them very little comfort in the moist mist from the sea. They talked about where they grew up, friends that they each might know, and food that they loved to eat, American and Arabic. Tahira laughed easily and it was difficult for Inayah to continue to see her as the terrorist she knew that the girl was. Women did not travel alone—anywhere. The woman should suspect her, as well, perhaps she did.

A roar went up from the crowd as the doors opened. Inayah's eyes scanned the crowd. She knew she had to get up to the front to get a clear shot at the target. As they entered she saw him standing on a platform by a microphone. She was so close! She squeezed her eyes tightly shut. *I must complete this.* She looked around the room as she wondered if Eitan would also be there.

"Welcome! Welcome everyone." An Arabic tongue spoke on the loud speaker. "We are all gathered here this morning to welcome our distinguished guest." Inayah began to squeeze her body towards the front. Tahira followed tightly behind her. They were only three rows behind the stage. She knew she could throw a knife from here and undoubtedly kill him fairly quickly, but she wanted to be sure. She would have to get closer. Again, as Inayah made her way expertly through the crowd, Tahira equally made her way through. Expert training or just very good at following?

Inayah's eyes looked at the target. He was looking out at the crowd with a smile on his face. She wanted to freeze his smile and then move out of the room. She looked at the exits. Both of them were difficult to reach due to the crowds and the guards. She stood on her tiptoes trying to decipher if she could kill him with a knife and then disappear through the curtains behind him. The problem was she didn't know what was behind those curtains. If she utilized her gun, it would make a lot of noise and people would panic instantly. A knife would be limited, with also, the realization that the knifing probably wouldn't give her enough time to exit unharmed. She felt for the knife on her thigh. All she had to do was throw it accurately at his chest or even between his black olive pit eyes and hope that she could move through the crowd fast enough to make a clean escape.

Inayah held her breath. This was the moment. All she had to do was reach and throw. She felt something against her back. She turned her head to see Tahira. "Sorry, I didn't mean to stick my elbow in your back." The young woman pushed up against Inayah's back. Inayah released her hold on her knife and eased it back into its sheath.

"Aren't you excited? We are here in presence. Just look at him and tell me you see a terrorist. Of course he is not!" The young woman squealed.

Inayah looked into the woman's eyes. Now she had to kill two people. For that she could use her gun and employ the stampeding people to her advantage. The target was waving his hand in the air as he spoke. Now or never, she thought. She touched the butt of her gun with one hand and the knife with her other. Without another thought the knife flew through the air and caught the target between his eyes, sliding deep to the handle. His hands went to pull it out and then fell limp at his sides. He tottered and fell over at the same time the shot rang out and blew a small hole in Tahira's chest. The woman's body fell back, but the crowd was so tightly packed that she did not fall down. The crowd began to scream and try to turn and run. Inayah looked at the stage and hurried to climb the stairs to go to the target's body to make sure he was dead. She yanked out her knife and wiped the crimson blood on the man's chest. He was definitely dead. She saw a small group of men rushing towards the body, as she slid through the stage curtains. As soon as she slid through the curtains she ran into a solid wall of a warm body.

"There you are." A deep voice resonated towards her. "Remember me?" She pushed her knife towards the man. He grabbed her wrist, "Now that's not very nice, is it?" His thumb pushed into her wrist, cracking her delicate wrist bones until she dropped the knife. "Now that's better. Come with me. I wouldn't want Ali Bababa's men to dice and quarter you before I get a chance to speak with you." He smiled. The man's head was covered with a checkered cloth. His beard was black and curled to his chest. She continued to race through the files of her brain trying to figure out where she knew this tall Arab man from. He pushed her through the crowd as they were scrambling toward the exits. He was calm and controlled. Inayah held her wrist in the palm of her other hand as she tried to ignore the throbbing pain. She knew she had to get away from him, but how? The crowd pushed around her, limiting her ability to plan an exit. She had no gun and she had no knife. Though she did have her legs, she quickly kicked the person on her right and threw her in front of her, then she kicked the next person and threw him at the woman she had just kicked. She continued to kick, as hard as she could, until she had made her way through six people and left them piled on each other. She saw the eyes of the captor flashing in anger, but continued to push and shove, until she got to the exit.

She rammed through the door and out into the parking lot where hundreds of people were also running.   Police   cars   were   arriving   and ambulances.   She hurried through the crowd. When she got behind a tree, she tore off her niqab and began to run down the street. She didn't look back until she had traversed at least ten blocks from the mayhem scene. She slid between two buildings so that she could observe if she was being followed. Her eyes scanned the sidewalk. No one was following her. She looked at her swollen wrist. She would need a doctor. She glanced at the cars parked along the road, searching for one with keys left in the ignition. It didn't take long before she found an old Volkswagon. She jumped inside and turned on the ignition and pulled out into traffic. She turned the car south on the 101, headed toward LAX airport.

She parked in self-park and made her way inside the airport. She headed to the small shops to buy herself a change of clothes.   Then she headed toward a pharmacy. She snatched a box of hair dye off the shelf. She grabbed at eyeliner, lipstick, and lash thickner and pulled a hairbrush out of large bin. She paid and then, she walked slowly down the long hallway to the women's rest room and showers.

When she emerged from the rest room, she had reddish blond hair, her eyes were outlined by soft brown liner, her brows matched her hair, and her lips were a soft pink. She went to the lost and found.

"Excuse me. I've lost my passport and my ticket. I had it when I went to the rest room. I think perhaps someone has stolen it out of my purse. My flight is leaving in forty minutes and..."

The man behind the counter pushed his glasses up on his nose. "I'm so sorry. What country are you from?"

"I was born in San Francisco, right here in California. I'm supposed to go to visit my sister in New Zealand. I don't know what I'm going to do."

The man surveyed her with a look of calculated interest. "Why don't you go into that little room right behind that blue door there and I will get someone to help you."

She nodded and went through the blue door and into the room that the man was pointing to. She sat at a long table, her throbbing wrist was covered with a tightly bound wrap, but hidden behind the long sleeve of her sweater.

A man popped into the room. "Hello Miss. I was told you lost your passport and your ticket to New Zealand. I'm so sorry to hear that. I may be able to help you."

The man interviewed her quite extensively. She had to fill out countless stacks of papers— home addresses, names of relatives. She had trained for this and memorized locales that she could utilize. She answered him effortlessly and wrote out each sheet perfectly. Then, he stood up and smiled, "Wait here a few moments." The man hurried out the door. She looked up at the clock. Thirty minutes left until her flight would leave. She felt exposed and naked without her niqab. She glanced at the corners of the room where cameras recorded her every move. This was it then, the end of the line. She imagined armed officers storming the room and carrying her away. Normally, she would have fought to her death, but her hand rested protectively on her stomach. The time for fighting was over.

The man popped back into the room. "Well, you are in luck. Our staff in security has cleared you, but unfortunately, you will have to purchase another ticket. It will take quite a few days for us to do the research on the ticket and get your money back to you, but all will be fine, I'm sure. I believe they are giving you a temporary Visa and a passport. Of course, you will have to apply to the American Embassy when you get there." He smiled and reached out and patted her hand that was resting on the table, her other hand was still gently laying across her stomach. "So, you better go to the reservation desk. They have been notified and you can then board immediately. I believe your plane has already boarded."

She blinked her dark eyes and cast them downward, "Thank you sir, thank you so much."

The man watched as she purchased her ticket. His eyes stayed glued to her as she went hurriedly down the boarding tunnel. He turned to the plain-clothed man in a seat by the door, resting his hand lightly on the man's shoulder he ordered, "Watch her closely. She's our only lead." The man in the brown suit stood up and went down the tunnel to board the plane and take his seat by the emergency door. He could see her very well, sitting in her aisle seat across from him, adjusting her seat to its upright position, patting her golden hair as she tried to make herself more presentable. The door hatch was closed. The plane began to taxi out onto the tarmac, but he never let his eyes wander away from her. He saw her hand grip the armrest and then release it. She was obviously uncomfortable. He watched her touch her own stomach several times, then grip the armrest again. When the plane lifted up into the air, he saw her lips form a perfect O as she inhaled and then exhaled deeply. It was only then that he saw her release her grip on the armrest, push the button on the seat to recline and shut her eyes. Maybe she wasn't the woman they thought she was. Maybe they followed the wrong woman. It was obvious to him that this woman had no desire to take over a plane, nor did she appear to be a terrorist ready to make a move. On the contrary, she appeared to be exactly who she said she was, a woman who had lost her passport and ticket and was going to see her sister in New Zealand. She didn't fit any profile of a terrorist, even in the most remote sense.

The man pushed his recline button and leaned back, but he kept his eyes on her. Yes, she was good, very good; that was exactly why he knew that he was trailing the right woman, the best professional female that he had ever tailed. Yet, there was something about her that wasn't quite right. He sensed it, but couldn't quite put his finger on what it was, but he didn't have to worry about her escaping him up here at 25,000 feet. It had been a long night. He glanced down at the few drops of blood that had splashed on his shirt. The guy had been difficult to break, but he finally had gotten what he wanted. There she was, not two feet from him, the notorious Inayah, the woman who had masterminded the assasination of the president. He could see the headlines that would be stamped on all the papers and would be splashed across the Internet: FBI Agent Tom Adams captures illusive female terrorist ,thwarting her escape to New Zealand. He sighed. It was a perfect ending to his thirty- year career. He would go out on top, a success with a big financial bonus to boot! He couldn't have written it any better if he had scripted his own life.

She kept her eyes closed, but one eye was cracked open just enough to watch the man across the aisle. Who was he? She knew he was following her. Perhaps just as an airport precaution, since they had let her on the plane without a valid passport, but her thoughts tormented her. Why would the airport let her on the plane without a valid passport? No, it all had been too easy; this man had an agenda. He was following her and his goal undoubtedly was to capture her, she was sure of that. He reeked of FBI. She got up to go to the rest room. He sensed she was up, but did not open his eyes. She stumbled and fell against him, "Oh, I'm so sorry!" She apologized as his eyes snapped open to look directly at her. She continued down the aisle to the restroom in the back of the plane. She turned to see if he was still watching her and of course, he was. She slipped into the bathroom to wait.   Ten minutes later she emerged. She walked down the narrow aisle back to her seat. She glanced at the man sleeping in the aisle seat across from hers. He was in an undeniable deep sleep. The FBI agent was dead...

When the plane landed she stood and calmly smiled at the attendant. She walked out of the plane slowly and appeared as if she was looking for someone. She continued to feign that she was looking for someone as she walked through the airport, turning her head left and right and pausing to look at the people gathered with signs waiting for loved ones or business partners, she heard, "Welcome to Auckland International Airport" over the loud speaker, over and over, until she got to the exit doors. Then, she slipped through the doors quickly, hurried across the boulevard, looking for a rental car agency shuttle. She saw the sign: About New Zealand Rental Cars and hopped on the shuttle.

She drove the rental car to the next rental car agency, leaving the rental car parked on the side of the road. She rented another car and hurriedly left. She kept her eyes peeled for anyone following her, but she could see in the rearview mirror that no car was tailing her. She sped through the streets, anxious for another mode of transportation. Rental cars were too easily traced and she didn't like to use them. There was always that "face" behind the counter that could identify her, even though she now had shortened blond hair. They had found her with that short blond hair. She knew she had to either get on a bus or a train in order to get lost in the maze and life shuffle of other people, which would be her true protection. She slid the car into a parking space and began to walk briskly. She glanced left and right and occasionally turned her body entirely in a circle, making sure that she was not being followed.

She turned on her cell phone and clicked on a walking map. She needed to get to the Britomart Transport Centre on 12 Queen Street, City Centre. Once there she could easily blend in with the people and lose herself in the crowd. She sat down on a bench where she could see any approaching stranger. She turned on her cell phone and looked up, Joe Everton. She had no other place to go. He was the one person Eiton had told her they could count on in New Zealand who wasn't attached to any agency.

Chapter 21

Months later, Inayah sat on a white cane chair on Joe Everton's porch over-looking Lake Hawea Station on the eastern shore. She sat sipping a glass of ice cold tea, munching on a meat pie, as she stared at the awesome, almost over-powering Grandview Mountain Range. Eitan's friend, Joe, had proved a true friend and more importantly than that, he was a "normal" friend without attachments to any government agency, other than his deepest desire to be a conservationist. Joe boasted about his boundary fencing of the 6,505 hectares of freehold land on Timaru Creek Road that was encircled by thousands of hectares of Crown controlled conservation land. He meticulously put out salt licks for the wild deer, as he marveled about the Chamois, which is an alpine antelope,and the abundance of trout which he enjoyed procuring from the eight kilometers of lake front. He enjoyed talking about all the wildlife and his responsibility to it. He rarely spoke of his relationship with Eitan. When she called him, at first he was stand offish, not giving her much information, but when she told him that she was Eitan's wife, he opened his doors to her and in many ways, also his heart. When he saw her belly growing with each passing day, he became concerned with her living so high in the mountains, even though Inayah assured him that babies are born every day in the mountains.

Joe was older and very rich, but looking at him one would guess him to be much younger than he appeared and might even guess that he was struggling to make a living as a farmer, which would be the farthest thing from the truth.

Joe kept her stomach filled with delicious trout and fried potatoes, as well as his expertly made meat pies with mushrooms, cheese and gravy and his delicious kiwi pie. He became quite close to Ina and would often tease and joke with her, pulling gently on his own grey moustache as he spoke. "You know I could have won the Bakels New Zealand Supreme Pie Award, but a person can't win. Has to be those pie manufacturers."

With her mouth full of unchewed meat pie she said, "Of course you would have to win, your pies are outstanding! This baby is going to be one little healthy fat dumpling with me eating all your delicious delights."

He smiled and patted her hand, "Of course it will be." She thought she saw his eyes fill with tears. Joe had hoped that his friend, Eitan, would have returned for his darling wife by now, but he stopped checking in town and he glanced less into the woods seeking an emerging tunic. "When the time for the baby gets closer I am going to drive you into the town hospital. It won't do to have the baby born way out here, that's for sure."

"Now Joe, we have discussed this before. I am quite capable of having a baby by myself out here in the wilderness. In fact, I prefer it." She didn't tell him that she didn't want to be recognized by someone in the town. She doubt if it would happen, but it could, and that would put the baby in danger. She hadn't left the ranch since he brought her here and she had no plans to do so. In truth, she had strapped one of his knives to her thigh, but she rarely even thought about it anymore.

"We will talk about it more later when your time gets closer." The one topic that they both yearned for was Eitan, but neither of them brought up his name. To do so would mean that they had to deal with his state of living or dead and neither of them was ready to deal with that reality.

She did not tell him of her life and he told her very little of his. The one thing that was apparent to her was that he was very rich, but didn't flaunt it in any manner. She liked his gentle touch and his soft deep voice. He would be the perfect grandfather for their child.

He looked deep into the forest, seeing the movement of brown. "Deer out there, right there on the right."

She peered straight ahead trying to see it, too. She saw the movement in the woods, but immediately knew that it was not a deer. Her hand reached out and gripped his hand tightly. "Joe, that's not a deer. There's someone in the woods." She put her hand over her eyes and looked out,

"No, there is more than one person out there. Do you ever see people on your land like this, Joe?"

He stood and shook his head, "No, those are trespassers. Go into the house Ina. Go upstairs and get into one of the closets and do not come out until I tell you, is that clear?"

She stood up and her big belly loomed in front of her awkwardly. She placed her hand on the hard bulge as the infant's elbow or foot moved along her skin. "I could help you. I'm a good fighter. Who do you think it is?" She felt her knife pushing against her thigh, with an urgency which she hadn't felt in a long time, not since the day she came to Joe's ranch. Her knife had been silent against her leg, not demanding any attention, but now it screamed out at her and she hated that feeling, more than anything. He shook his head, "No, go upstairs." He growled. She obeyed his orders and went upstairs, but she didn't get into the closet. For one, it reminded her too much of the time with her mother years ago, but also she needed to be ready to leave if she had to. She had to protect her baby. She checked the windows on the back side of the house and opened one of them for a fast escape. Then, she went back to the front and watched and waited. She could no longer see anyone in the woods. She watched Joe on the porch as he slowly put bullets into the barrel of a gun. Maybe she was wrong about Joe. Maybe he had worked with Eitan, maybe he knew who they were and what they did. Maybe he lived out here in the outback of New Zealand because he was hiding just like she was. Maybe he was done with that life and came here to find peace at last. She watched as he hid behind one of the stone pillars on the porch. She wished that she had a gun. Her eyes scanned the woods. Nothing.

Then, on the right side of the picturesque landscape she saw movement. The camouflaged-suited man moved from one tree to a closer tree. He raised his gun and aimed. She heard the bullet hit the side of the house. Then she saw three of them beginning to rush towards the house. Joe raised his gun and shot through one head and then another. There was one sniper left. The man began to shoot a volley at Joe. Inayah's body became rigid. She knew that Joe was in trouble when she saw three more camouflaged men emerge from the tree line. She hurried out of the room and down the stairs. She couldn't let him be overrun.

"Joe! There's three more!" He glanced up and threw her a pistol. She caught the small revolver in the palm of her hand. She felt the cold steel in her hand and instantly her pupils narrowed. She raised the gun and shot at one of the men running towards them. She shot again and watched as his body dove into the grass. She waited to see if he moved, but she knew he wouldn't. She had shot him right between his eyes.

"Stay down, Ina!" Joe shouted as he shot towards the remaining three intruders. She took aim, but the man jumped to the side and the bullet caught the man's right shoulder. She shot again and the bullet went through his upper thigh. He hollered out in pain as he fell into the grass. The other two continued to advance. Joe shot the remainder of his bullets, but they missed their target. Inayah felt a strange sensation in her body, something she had never felt before. She could even taste it in her mouth, a dry, bitter bile taste.

She felt absolute terror. She put her hand on her protruding stomach and said a prayer. She raised the gun and aimed as one of the men jumped not six feet from her. The bullet bored into the man's face and he fell backward. Inayah turned toward Joe, "Only one more Joe. Do you see him?" Joe did not answer. He lay on the porch with a perfect round red dot in his forehead. "No," she whispered. "Oh Joe, no." She began to breathe heavily, searching the tree line for the last man. She listened for his footsteps, for any rustle of leaves or a snap of a twig, but heard nothing. She leaned against the rock pillar on the porch and strained her eyes. Where could he be? She tried to control her breathing, but her air exited her mouth in quick fearful puffs. She leaned back, but her stomach was exposed a mere two inches beyond the pillar. If he was there, he would see it. He would aim for it and the bullet would kill her child. She moved towards the back of the porch and then through the front door. She ran up the stairs, glancing backwards every few seconds. She went into the room that she had opened the window for her escape. She locked the door.

Inayah waited. She crouched next to the door, listening for the creaking of floor boards, but she heard nothing. She leaned her head against the wooden door, holding the pistol ready. She felt her child turning within her, squirming and moving, trying to feel secure again. She placed her hand against the taunt skin and patted gently. "Don't worry." She whispered, more for herself than for her baby. She glanced at the window. The curtains were blowing into the room with the breeze that had just began to stir. Then, she heard the unmistakable creaking of the stairs. She steadied the gun in her hand. He would kick open the door, it would swing away from her and she would have a clear shot. She waited. She heard the doorknob turn, but the door was locked. He had to kick it in. She saw the knob turn and stop one way and then turn and stop the other way. She heard the blast of a gun and then the door burst open. She rolled onto her side and shot five times into the space where the intruder's body was supposed to appear.

There was no one in the doorway.

Her breath puffed in and out of her nose in rapid succession as she hyper-ventilated with her fear. She knew she had one more bullet. She waited. If she moved he would know where she was and shoot at her, undoubtedly killing her and her child. She felt a tear forming in her left eye. A tear? She would laugh, if she wasn't so afraid for her infant's life. When had she last cried tears? She couldn't remember. Real tears, not crocodile fake tears. She quickly searched her memory and couldn't remember a single time, yet she was sure there was a time. Hadn't there been a time when she was still human? Then, she remembered. She had cried when she ordered the murder of the American president and all those people, but she never cried again after that, until now. Now, an uncontrolled tear zigzagged down her cheek and hit the wooden floor in front of her, creating a small round wet drop.

She saw movement in front of her and quickly shot the last bullet, barely grazing the intruder's hip, but he fell on the wooden floor in front of her, covering her one tear drop on the floor with his body. He lifted up on his arm and his eyes zeroed in on hers. She slid her knife from its sheath and brought it down quickly through his skull—again and again and again.

She tried to stand, but slipped in the puddle of his warm crimson blood. Her hand slid across the floor, leaving a perfect print of her fingers in its wake. She managed to push herself to a standing position and stood in the growing puddle of blood, staring down at the man who had almost taken her child's life. She moved along the wall until she got to the door's opening and then she slid out, the bright red knife still tightly clutched in her hand. She inched down the stairs, her back tightly to the wall, her hands leaving their bright fingers on the paint as she moved slowly to the bottom. She moved onto the porch, grabbed the dead man's automatic weapon, and then made her way out into the yard. She began to move toward the mountain behind the house, away from the treeline, away from the lake. Her feet hit the ground in solid thumps as she hurried as fast as she could, but she was aware that it was more like a waddle away to freedom. She didn't look back towards the house, but kept her pace until she was at the edge of the mountain. She knew she couldn't climb it, but she could hike around it. She would find shelter for the night and then make a plan. She heard a twig snap and turned with her gun pointed and ready, but it was too late, the new intruder grabbed her arm and turned her toward him. "Sweetheart, it's me!" She saw his face, she heard his voice, but she still did not allow herself to recognize her husband. She began to struggle to try to pull away. "Inayah! Stop! It's me my darling." He pulled her close and wrapped her tightly in his arms. "Sweetheart, it's over. You and the baby are safe." She struggled for a moment longer and then relaxed in his arms.

"Eitan, it IS you. You are alive."

"Yes my love, I am alive. Are you alright?"

She shook her head, "Oh Eitan, Joe is dead. Poor Joe is dead."

He held her even more tightly. "We have to hurry my love. There is a boat on the lake so that we can make our get away. Everything is going to be alright now my love. No more ISIS, no more Mossad. We are going deep into the outback where we can safely raise our baby. I love you darling."

Her eyes filled with tears and spilled down her cheeks. She put her hands on her stomach. "The three of us?"

"Forever my sweet. No more running. No more fighting."

She allowed him to hold onto her elbow as he guided her toward the lake. She could see the small boat bobbing along the shoreline. She had so many questions, but she didn't need them answered now. They were all together again and nothing else mattered. He helped her onto the boat and started the engine. He slipped his arm around her. "You are safe now darling. I promise you." The boat backed out into the water.

"Is this a forever- after ending?" She smiled at him. He caressed her cheek with the back of his hand.

"Yes my sweet Inayah, this is our forever-after ending. You and I and our child."

"Forever?" She asked like a child wanting everything to fall into place, everything to be neat and tidy and predictable.

"Yes my sweet, forever."

Inayah knew *forever* was a lie, but she was willing to accept his words for now, even as her eyes caught the glint of the barrel of a gun coming out of the woods. She inhaled deeply and pursed her lips tightly together. *Nothing is going to spoil my forever,* she thought. She tilted her face up for Eitan to kiss her. He pressed his lips on hers and pulled her as close to his body as he could, in his futile attempt to convey that this moment was the beginning of their *forever*...

*****

www.ingramcontent.com/pod-product-compliance
Lightning Source LLC
Chambersburg PA
CBHW031610240626
47153CB00002B/704